Shake-It-Up Tales!

"An essential tool for librarians
looking for participation tales from
different cultures...a great resource."
—*School Library Journal*

"...excellent resource for beginners...
valuable tool for more experienced tellers as well."
—*The Bulletin of the Center for Children's Books*

"...helpful for librarians, teachers,
caregivers, or family members
who tell stories to young children."
—*VOYA*

Shake-It-Up Tales!
Stories to Sing, Dance, Drum, and Act Out

Margaret Read MacDonald

With help from Jen and Nat Whitman, Wajuppa Tossa, and the Mahasarakham Storytellers.

August House Publishers, Inc.
LITTLE ROCK

Published 2000 by August House Publishers, Inc.,
P.O. Box 3223, Little Rock, Arkansas, 72203, 501-372-5450.

Printed in the United States of America

10 9 8 7 6 5 4 3 2   HB
10 9 8 7 6 5 4 3   PB

LIBRARY OF CONGRESS CATALOGING-IN-PUBLICATION DATA
MacDonald, Margaret Read, 1940–
    Shake-it-up tales! : stories to sing, dance, drum, and act out / Margaret Read MacDonald.
        p. cm.
    "With help from Jen and Nat Whitman, Wajuppa Tossa, and the Mahasarakham Storytellers."
    Includes bibliographical references.
    ISBN 0–87483–590–9 (alk. paper) — ISBN 0–87483–570–4 (pbk. : alk. paper)
    1. Storytelling—United States. 2. Tales. 3. Activity programs in education—United States. I.
        Title.

LB1042.M228 2000
372.67'7—dc21   00-036228

Executive editor: Liz Parkhurst
Project editor: Joy Freeman
Manuscript editor: Bill Jones
Cover design: Patrick McKelvey

The paper used in this publication meets the minimum requirements
of the American National Standard for Information Sciences—
Permanence of Paper for Printed Library Materials, ANSI Z39.48-1984.

AUGUST HOUSE   PUBLISHERS   LITTLE ROCK

Contents

DRAMATIC PLAY

Acknowledgments

MY THANKS TO TELLERS RAOUF MAMA AND
Lynn Moroney for allowing me to retell their stories for this book. I
give complete citations for their work with those stories, and hope you
will consult their originals as well as my "easy-to-tell" retellings.

In the past few years my storytelling life has been complicated and
enriched by others. Working in Thailand alongside Dr. Wajuppa Tossa,
we developed simultaneous storytelling techniques that were in
essence telling in tandem. And touring throughout Isaan with our
Mahasarakham Storytelling Troupe we found ourselves relying on
tandem telling and story theatre to develop pieces that our students
could perform successfully before six hundred elementary children in
a hot, dusty outdoor stage setting. Some of the stories included here
were shaped by our students through several months of performances.
So I owe thanks to all members of the Mahasarakham Storytelling
Troupe.

During my second winter in Thailand, Jim Wolf, an itinerant teller
from Boone, North Carolina, joined us. Jim delighted our audiences
with his laid-back, gentle tellings. He seemed to almost dance his
stories at times. The fact that all was being translated simultaneously
by Prasong Saihong probably encouraged Jim to use much more
action and fewer words. I learned a great deal about audience trust
while watching him work with our children. So thanks to Jim for his
presence and for one of his stories included here.

At Christmas my daughter, Jen, and her husband, Nat Whitman,
arrived for vacation and immediately joined us on tour. They quickly
picked up the tandem-telling routine, and within a year had developed
their own tandem repertoire and were performing in libraries back
home in Seattle. As I coached them in each season's tour and even
joined in a few of their performances, I was influenced strongly by
their own theater-inspired style. Several of the stories here were first
developed by the Whitmans or were strongly shaped by their performances. So thanks to Nat and Jen for letting Mom play with you!

Learning to let loose of the story a bit, discovering the joy of sharing the tale with another, I am now ready to play story with a musician friend, Richard Scholz. Richard provides a musical background to my telling, but can be persuaded to chime in with a bit of tandem telling, too, at times. So Richard's hand can be seen in some of these tales as well.

All of these folks, plus several other energetic translator-tellers with whom I have worked, have helped move my style into an increasingly playful mode. For years I have called my workshops "Playing with Story" and had hoped to call this book *Story Play*. But my editor, Liz Parkhurst, convinced me that we needed to go a step further and title this one *Shake-It-Up Tales*!

Note: Motif-index references in tale notes refer to *The Storyteller's Sourcebook: A Subject, Title, and Motif Index to Folklore Collections for Children* by Margaret Read MacDonald (Gale Research, 1982) and to *The Storyteller's Sourcebook, Volume 2* by Margaret Read MacDonald and Brian Sturm (Gale Research, 2000). Type index references are for *The Types of the Folktale* by Antti Aarne and Stith Thompson (Helsinki: Suomalainen Tiedeakatemia, Academia Scientiarum Fennica, 1973).

1 Playing with Story

THE USE OF STORY WITH CHILDREN AND ADULTS CAN BE joyous, playful, a moment of release. There is a time for quiet, thoughtful tales, yes. But in this book I present stories to which you can bounce, sing, and dance. I want you to get your audience on their feet. Involve them. *Enjoy* them. Play together.

Whether you are a parent, teacher, or freelancing storyteller, there is something here for you. Find a story you like. Gather an audience. And play with story!

A word to parents:

Story play in the home can be as simple or as elaborate as you want to make it. The important thing is that you enjoy sharing the story and "playing it" with your children. After you have read or told the story, let your children choose roles and act it out as you retell or assist. Once the children have claimed ownership of their favorite tales, they will enjoy acting them out even when you are not around. But a modeling of story play can get them started on this imaginative activity.

Though our discussions of story activities will often assume a group of children, keep in mind that all of these story play ideas are just as much fun when adapted for two or three kids on a lazy summer day on the lawn.

A word to teachers, librarians, and group leaders:

In cultures where story is a regular part of family and community life, story often expands into a playful shared experience with all ages joining in. The same story is told over and over, and soon everyone knows all the parts. Audiences can join in on the songs and chants or jump up to act out parts of the story. This playful release in story play is a joy our audiences, too, should experience. In this story collection,

I include tales that allow for easy expansion into audience participation, story theatre, and group drama. I am not suggesting that you "put on a play," though folktales are perfect vehicles to stage. I do suggest that you involve your audience in chanting, singing, and drumming during your story. At times it is fun to follow your story with a retelling in which children join physically in moving about the room and acting out the tale.

In this book:

We include in this book twenty stories for your use. Notes are also given for others that make great audience participation or group drama tales. We also list story collections, audio-tapes, and videos of tellers. These help locate material you can have fun playing with. They also present telling styles that might inspire as you develop your own "playing with story" skills.

You will find first tales for "Chanting, Singing, Dancing, Drumming." There is a chapter of simple audience participation "Chants, Claps, Motions, and Sound Effects." And we have chapters for "Singing Tales," "Drumming Tales," and "Dancing Tales."

In our second section you will find "Talk-Back Tales." Here are stories that allow the audience to contribute to the telling. A chapter on "Stories with Improv Slots" offers tales in which the audience contributes suggestions that help direct the story. "Riddle Stories" let the audience venture guesses during the telling.

Our "Dramatic Play" section takes audience participation a step further with an "Actors-from-the-Audience" chapter. We suggest ways in which you might present stories with a partner or a group as "Tandem Telling" or "Story Theatre." And we include "Act-It-Out-Tales" for an easy creative dramatic follow-up to your storytelling.

On learning tales from a printed text:

The stories in this book are presented in a style folklorists call "ethnopoetic transcription." This simply means that the stories are set on the page in a format designed to evoke the spoken telling. Wherever I pause in my telling, the text line breaks. This helps you feel the pacing of the story. Because I have told these stories many times and let many audiences help me shape them, they are fairly tellable by now. Beginning tellers can often find easy success by sticking close to the shaped tales of other tellers. You will find my lists of "more stories to tell" here refer often to stories from other of my storytelling collections and to collections by tellers such as Diane Wolkstein, Moses Serawadda, and Anne Pellowski. Because we have told these stories over and over again we have done much of your work for you. You can begin with a text that should work for your audiences.

However, you need not feel constricted by the printed words of these tale texts. These are *folk* tales. Every person who ever passed on a folktale changed it to suit his or her own persona. Even one teller seldom tells a tale exactly the same way twice. Once you have chosen a story to learn from this book, read the tale aloud a few times. Let the words and the flow of the story sink into you. Learn the songs or chants. Then put the book away, and just tell the story in your own words. Play with it. Make it your own. From now on it is *your* story, and any way you tell it is exactly the *right* way.

The songs within these stories are *folk*-songs. They, too, change with each use. So don't be intimidated by the lovely singing voices you might hear on tellers' tapes. If you can't recall the tune exactly, sing it any way you like, or even make up your own. That is what storytellers have always done. Don't worry about it. Just create a playful whole of story and song and tell the tale!

On telling these stories:

Of the many reasons why one should tell stories, I find most appealing the simple fact that through story we can share the joy of creating together an artistic moment. In story play, the audience gets to become a part of this act of creation. It is their involvement, their enthusiasm, their vocal and physical additions to the telling that make the story such fun. They sense this and feel a joyous pride in the story event we create together.

In this book, I will suggest several ways to involve your audiences in such story play. Possibilities range from the simple induced audience cheer to a staged telling with improvisational actors snatched from the audience. These varying techniques will be discussed chapter by chapter.

A few points to consider when telling these tales. Trust your story, trust your face, trust your body. The audience needs one thing from you...a sense that you *care* for them. It is your face, your body, your voice that convey this. Do not distract them from your being by poking puppets at them, cloaking yourself in bizarre costumery, or other tomfoolery. Twirling batons and flashing flags are not needed. The teller must not push at the audience with flashy attention-getting devices in attempts to attract them. If the teller's persona is not attractive in its simplicity, all the sequins in the world will not make a difference. And the teller must not be concerned with parading teller skills for approval. An audience can swiftly guess that a teller is more interested in impressing than in providing them with a fine tale, and their interest in the teller's words dims.

The audience needs *you* and their sense that you are reaching out to them. They simply need a teller who is *there in the moment* for them. The teller must be focused on *caring* for this audience, catering to their needs, eliciting their joys. You need not possess excessive dramatic skills for this. You need simply to *care*.

I do not want to imply by all this that one should never combine storytelling with other art forms. Certainly, if you are first a puppeteer, dancer, or singer and have come to story as an enhancement for your art, you will be combining story with that art. In Rio, I was enchanted by the work of Joaquim de Paula. He is a storytelling puppeteer. Beginning his story in traditional form, he will suddenly produce a large rod puppet and let it gracefully move the story forward through motion and voice. Just as easily, the puppet disappears and we are back into the magic of Joaquim's own voice and face. The puppets never upstage him. They never seem brought out to grab our attention. We are already rapt in the story. They appear simply to enhance our already seething imagination. But Joaquim is a skilled puppeteer and puppet maker. His ability to weave storytelling and puppetry into an artistic whole is unusual.

For the most part, I suggest that you keep your tellings simple and direct. Your job in sharing these lively pieces is to facilitate a shared experience of play for your audience. Rest assured that no telling is a *better* telling than the one you give from your heart to your own small group of children. Each teller is unique in his or her ability to share. Your telling will exist in that moment as a delight of story shaped by yourself and your audience.

Section One

Chanting, Singing, Dancing, Drumming

2 Chants, Claps, Motions, and Sound Effects

THOUGH ALL OF THE TECHNIQUES IN THIS BOOK ALLOW the audience to take part, this chapter will deal with the most common form of audience participation, the encouragement of simple verbal repetition and hand motions within the framework of a story. The stories utilizing this technique are usually folktales with a structure of repeated segments. In order for the audience to participate, listeners must be able to sense where they come in. Stories with repetition facilitate audience response.

Sometimes an audience will begin to join in on their own. Usually you will need to give them some cue indicating that you would like them to chime in. As you begin a refrain on which the audience could join, look the audience in the eye, nod encouragement and motion for them to chant or sing with you. You may want to give them a quick command, "Sing it with me!" or "Help me chant." As you rehearse the story, rehearse also the way you will bring your audience into participation. And rehearse the way you will silence their participation when the story needs to progress. Children sometimes become quite caught up in a particularly rollicking refrain and need to be brought to a stop with a firm hand when the interlude is finished.

You need to lead the audience skillfully so that their participation lends itself to the artistic whole of the telling experience. Never let the audience become so rousty in their participation that they distort the story. Never force an audience into participation if they really don't want to take part. With junior high and teen audiences in particular, you may meet entrenched resistance to participation. Invite a recalcitrant audience to participate, encourage them, but then let them listen quietly in peace if they really don't want to join in.

Examine your stories carefully to determine whether audience participation will add to the story experience or detract. There are stories that can be damaged by participation. Just because a refrain repeats does not mean the audience should be encouraged to join in. Consider the effect a chanting audience will have on the story. Does that sort of boisterous involvement move the story along and lift it, or does it sidetrack the tale from its meanings? I tell a story called "Strength" about a contest among animals. The refrain is one in which audiences often want to join, even without my encouragement. I have to be careful to not let them do this, because to do so would put the audience in control of the story's pacing. At the end of that story, the refrain has to flip quickly from humor to a very serious tone. With the audience chanting along I could not create this change.

Within a story there may be spots where you will want to encourage participation and spots where it is more effective to let the audience decide whether they want to chime in or not. In "Telesik," in our "Singing Tales" chapter, the little boy sings a rowing song. I want the audience to join on this and actively encourage them. There is also a song sung by Telesik's mother. There is a quiet, sweet tone to her song. Encouraging the audience to participate could alter this tone. However often they begin to sing along without my encouragement. If they do, I accept their participation here but am careful to direct them to quiet voices.

It will be useful for you to observe other tellers using audience-participation techniques. Toward this end, audio and video tapes are included in the bibliographies. For an instructive example of a teller eliciting simple audience response, see the video *Who Made This Mess* by Bill Harley (Hollywood: A & M Video, 1992), 52 min. Notice how he uses timing to gently entice the audience to join in on his repeated words.

All of the stories in this book call for audience participation. In this chapter I include those with the simplest form of participation…a repeated refrain or contributed sound effect.

More tales for
simple audience participation:

Caps for Sale by Esphyr Slobodkina (Harper & Row, 1940). An old favorite, children make motions with teller as monkeys mock the salesman. Easy to act out afterwards. For a variant of this story from Mali, see *The Hatseller and the Monkeys* by Baba Wagué Diakité (New York: Scholastic Press, 1999). Diakité heard this story from his father while growing up in a Fulani village.

"Cheese and Crackers" in *A Parent's Guide to Storytelling* by Margaret Read MacDonald (New York: HarperCollins, 1995), 52–61. Audience joins family members who run off to store chanting, "Cheese and crackers." Old Bear stops each. Variant of the well known tale, "Sody Sallerytus."

Did You Feed My Cow? by Margaret Taylor (New York: Thomas Crowell, 1969), 17–18, and in *A Second Storyteller's Choice* by Eileen Colwell (New York: Henry Z. Walck, 1965), 57–58. Call-and-response chant.

"Drakestail" in *Fireside Stories* by Veronica S. Hutchinson (New York: Minton & Balch, 1927), 51–66. Children quack with Drakestail, "Quack, Quack, Quack! I want my money back!"

"The Freedom Bird" by David Holt in *Ready-to-Tell Tales* by David Holt and Bill Mooney (Little Rock: August House, 1994), 219–22. Bird taunts hunter. Audience joins in bird's mocking chant.

Fortunately by Remy Charlip (New York: Aladdin Books, 1953). Audience repeats refrains "That's good" and "That's bad" as fate flip flops.

"Gecko" in *The Storyteller's Start-Up Book* by Margaret Read MacDonald (Little Rock: August House, 1993), 139–46. Audience chants with animals as each stomps in an attempt to reach water.

"The Hobyahs" in *More English Folk and Fairy Tales* by Joseph Jacobs (New York: Putnam, 1894), 127–33. Also in *When the Lights Go Out* by Margaret Read MacDonald (New York: H.W. Wilson, 1988), 96–103. Little Dog Turpie barks and scares off the fearful hobyahs each night. Audience repeats the Hobyah's fearful call, "Hobyah! Hobyah! Hobyah!" Fun and silly as I tell it, but not for the faint of heart. Tell the gory version or don't tell it at all.

"Lifting the Sky" in *Peace Tales: World Folktales to Talk About* by Margaret Read MacDonald (Hamden, Conn.: Linnet, 1992), 82–84. Audience joins in shout as they push up the sky. From the repertoire of Upper Skagit teller Vi Hilbert. Hear her performance on *Coyote and Rock and Other Lushootseed Stories* (New York: Parabola/HarperCollins, 1992).

"The Old Woman and the Pig" in *Did You Feed My Cow?* by Margaret Taylor (New York: Thomas Y. Crowell, 1969), 20–21.

The Old Woman Who Lived in a Vinegar Bottle by Margaret Read MacDonald (Little Rock: August House, 1995). Old woman complains about her house. Audience whines with her. Fairy grants wishes. Audience repeats fairy's chants.

Slop! A Welsh Folktale by Margaret Read MacDonald, illus. by Yvonne LeBrun Davis (Golden, Colo.: Fulcrum Kids, 1997). Children help peel potatoes, carrots, onions and pour out bucket…"*Slop!*"

"The Tailor's Jacket" in *Earth Care: World Folktales to Talk About* by Margaret Read MacDonald (North Haven, Conn.: Linnet, 1999), 94–97. Audience snips and sews with the tailor. A more elaborate telling is "The Tailor" in *The Moral of the Story* by Bobby and Sherry Norfolk (Little Rock: August House, 1999), 49–58. For a singing version, hear *Tell It With Me* by Doug Lipman (Albany, N.Y.: A Gentle Wind, 1985).

"The Stepchild and the Fruit Trees" in *Singing Tales of Africa* by Adjai Robinson (New York: Scribner's, 1974), 24–33, and "Udala Tree" in *Twenty Tellable Tales* by Margaret Read MacDonald (New York: H.W. Wilson, 1986), 115–25. Audience joins in boy's tree-growing chant, "Udala fruit! Nda!"

"The Strange Visitor" in *English Folk and Fairy* Tales by Joseph Jacobs (New York: Putnam, n.d.), 186–89 and in When *the Lights Go Out* by Margaret Read MacDonald (New York: H.W. Wilson, 1988), 133–42. MacDonald's is very easy to tell, lots of audience repetition. Jacobs retains the marvelous wail, "Aihh late and wee moul!"

The Wedding Procession of the Rag Doll and the Broom Handle and Who Was In It by Carl Sandburg, illus. by Harriet Pincus (San Diego: Harcourt Brace Jovanovich, 1992). Let children make the motions of the marchers. After you tell it once, let everyone get up, assign parts, and have your own procession.

Collections with
audience-participation tales:

Crazy Gibberish and Other Story Hour Stretches by Naomi Baltuck (Hamden, Conn.: Linnet, 1993). See especially for the many participation songs and stretches. An accompanying audiotape is available if you need help with the tunes.

Fish with the Deep Sea Smile: Stories and Poems for Reading to Young Children by Virginia Tashjian (Hamden, Conn.: Linnet, 1988). Participation poems, songs, and stories.

The Ghost and I: Scary Stories for Participatory Telling ed. Jennifer Justice. (Cambridge, Mass.: Yellow Moon, 1992). See "The Ghost Hunt," "The Graveyard Voice," and more.

Here Comes the Storyteller by Joe Hayes (El Paso, Tex.: Cinco Puntos Press, 1996). See "Rain" (audience helps make storm and frog and locust chorus), "Válgame Dios!" (audience joins in Spanish refrain), "Yellow Corn Girl" (audience joins in grasshopper's song), "The Earth Monster" (audience joins in pretending to play rattles and drums and in singing to turn the Earth Monster to stone) and others. Tales with a Southwestern flavor.

Juba This and Juba That by Virginia Tashjian (Boston: Little Brown, 1995). See "Seven Little Rabbits" and other participatory poems and songs.

Len Cabral's Storytelling Book by Len Cabral and Mia Manduca (New York: Neal-Schuman, 1997). Margin notes discuss the way Len moves, speaks, and works with his audiences during the tellings. He discusses the use of audience participation and includes several useful stories for this technique. He does not cite sources for the stories he retells.

Listen and Help Tell the Story by Bernice Wells Carlson (New York: Abingdon, 1965). See the poetry here.

Look Back and See: Twenty Lively Tales for Gentle Tellers (New York: H. W. Wilson, 1991). See "Look Back and See" (audience huffs with climbers as they seek the dawn) and many singing tales.

The Storyteller's Start-Up Book by Margaret Read MacDonald (Little Rock: August House, 1993). See "Turtle of Koka," "The Little Old Woman Who Lived in a Vinegar Bottle," and others.

Twenty Tellable Tales by Margaret Read MacDonald (New York: H.W. Wilson, 1986). See "Little Crab and His Magic Eyes" (audience chants with crab as he sends his eyes sailing over the deep blue sea), "Old One-Eye" (audience scritch-scratches and rocks with old woman), "Parley Garfield and the Frogs" (audience helps with frog calls), "Little Rooster and the Turkish Sultan" (audience crows with rooster), "Jack and the Robbers" (audience slaps legs and helps characters jog along), and others.

The Terrible Nung Guama

A Folktale from China

An old woman lived all alone in a hut high on the mountain.
One day this old woman heard a terrible sound.
Something was coming down the mountain path.
It sounded like this:
>*Flup…Flup…Flup…Flup*

The old woman opened her door just a crack and peered out.

Coming down the path was a horrid creature!
It's head was as big as a rice basket.
It's body was big as a bull's.
It had long hair all over its body.
And its feet were huge…
they were floppy…
they made a squashing noise as it tromped through the mud.
>*Flup…Flup…Flup…Flup*

It *stopped*.
It snuffled.
It looked straight at the old woman.
Then it began to speak.
>"I am the Terrible Nung Guama!"
>Tonight I am coming to EAT YOU UP!"

Slowly it turned.
It walked back up the mountain.
>*Flup…Flup…Flup…Flup*

The old woman sat down on her step.
She began to wail:
>"The Terrible Nung Guama!
>The Terrible Nung Guama!
>The Terrible Nung Guama
>is coming to eat me up!"

Just then a peddler came by.
"What's this?
The Terrible Nung Guama?
He is a *bone cruncher*!
But perhaps I can help.
Take these needles.
Stick them all around your door.
When the Nung Guama comes,
it will prick its fingers on the needles.
Then maybe it will go away!"

"Oh *thank* you."
The old woman stuck the needles all around her door.
"When the Nung Guama comes,
it will prick its fingers on the needles.
Then maybe it will go away.
Maybe…
and maybe *not*!
The Terrible Nung Guama!
The Terrible Nung Guama!
The Terrible Nung Guama
is coming to eat me up!"

Just then a farmer came by carrying a basket of cow manure
    to put on his fields.
"Old woman, the *Terrible Nung Guama* is coming?
He is a *bone cruncher*!
But perhaps I can help.
Take this cow manure.
Spread it all around your door.
When the Nung Guama pricks its fingers,
it will get cow manure all over its hands, too.
Then maybe it will go away."

"Oh *thank* you."
The old woman spread the cow manure all over her door.
"Now when the Nung Guama comes
it will prick its fingers on the needles,
it will get cow manure all over its hands,
then maybe it will go away.
Maybe…
and maybe *not*!

The Terrible Nung Guama!
The Terrible Nung Guama!
The Terrible Nung Guama
is coming to eat me up!"

Just then a fishmonger came by with a basket of poison eels.
"The Terrible Nung Guama is coming?
He is a *bone cruncher*!
Perhaps I can help.
Put these poison eels in your water jar.
When the Nunga Guama gets manure on its hands,
it will go to the water jar to wash.
The poison eels will bite it.
Then maybe it will go away."

"Oh *thank* you!"
The old woman put the poison eels in her water jar.
"Now when the Nung Guama comes,
it will prick its fingers on the needles,
it will get cow manure on its hands,
it will go to the water jar to wash
and be bitten by the poisonous eels,
then maybe it will go away.
Maybe…
and maybe *not*!
The Terrible Nung Guama!
The Terrible Nung Guama!
The Terrible Nung Guama
is coming to eat me up!"

Here came the farmer's wife with a basket of eggs.
"What's this I hear?
The Terrible Nung Guama is coming!
But he is a *bone cruncher*!
Perhaps I can help.
Take these eggs and hide them in the warm ashes
    by the hearth.
When the Nung Guama is bitten by the poison eels,
it will rush to the hearth to rub ashes on the bites
    and stop the bleeding.
The eggs will explode in its eyes!
Then maybe it will go away."

"Oh *thank* you."
The old woman put the eggs in fireplace ashes.
"Now when the Nung Guama comes,
it will prick its fingers,
it will get manure on its hands,
it will rush to the water jar
and be bitten by eels,
it will go to the hearth to rub ashes on its bites,
and the eggs will explode in its face!
Then maybe it will go away.
Maybe…
and maybe *not*!"
The Terrible Nung Guama!
The Terrible Nung Guama!
The Terrible Nung Guama
is coming to eat me up!"

Here came the miller rolling a mill stone.
"What's this? The Nung Guama?
It is a *bone cruncher*!
Perhaps I can help.
Prop this mill stone on the frame over your bed.
When the Nung Guama is blinded by the exploding eggs
it will blunder around the room.
When it bumps into your bed,
the mill stone will fall down on its head,
and *do it in*!"

"Oh *thank* you."
The old woman propped the mill stone onto the frame
above her bed.
"Now when the Nung Guama comes,
it will prick its fingers on the needles.
It will get cow manure on its hands.
It will rush to wash in the water jar
and be bitten by the eels.
It will go to the hearth for ashes,
and the eggs will explode in its face.
It will blunder around the room
and bump into my bed.
The mill stone will fall down onto its head
and…*do it in*!
At last I can go to bed and go to *sleep*."

And the old woman went to bed.
But she didn't go to sleep.
When it was dark she heard a sound.
>Flup…Flup…Flup…Flup
Down the mountain path came the Terrible Nung Guama.
>Flup…Flup…Flup…
It came right up to her door.
It stopped.
It snuffled.
It smashed open the door.
>"Aaaaack!"
The needles pricked its fingers!
>"Aaaaack!"
The cow manure smeared its hands!
It ran to the water jar to wash.
>"Aaaaack!"
The poison eels bit its fingers!
It ran to the hearth to rub ashes on the wounds.
>"Aaaaack!"
The eggs exploded in the Nung Guama's eyes!
The Nung Guama blundered around the room.
It bumped into the old woman's bed.
>"Aaaaarrrggg!"
The millstone fell down onto the Nung Guama's head.
and *did it in*!

>"At last!"
The old woman got out of bed.
She picked up the Nung Guama by its great floppy feet
and dragged it out the door of her hut.
She dragged it to the edge of the mountain path,
and gave it one big *push*!
And off it rolled down the mountain.
>*Whup…Whup…Whup…*

The old woman went back inside.
She rolled out the millstone.
She swept up her hearth.
She went to bed and she went to sleep.
And in the morning that old woman went to town
and bought herself a strong new door,
and a fine brass lock to *keep it shut*.

Tips for telling:

It is, of course, great fun to get the audience chanting with you on the "flup…flup…flup…flup." Sometimes we slap our legs also, making a fluppy sound.

About the story:

This tale is elaborated from "The tale of Nung-kua-ma" in *Folktales of China* by Wolfram Eberhard (Chicago: University of Chicago, 1965), 143–46. Eberhard collected over twenty-six texts of this story in China. He labels it Type *130 The Animals in Night Quarters* and Type *210 Cock, Hen, Duck, Pin and Needle on a Journey*. He notes that the *Types of Indic Oral Tales* cites twelve versions of this tale. This is also Motif *K1161 Animals hidden in various parts of a house attack owner with their characteristic powers and kill him when he enters.* You might recognize the motif in this story as that in "The Bremen Town Musicians." In many Asian variants the tale is told of an old woman living alone. MacDonald's *Storyteller's Sourcebook* lists variants from China, Pakistan, Korea, and Bengal. An interesting picture book version with illustrations by Ed Young was published in 1978 by Collins & World and the U.S. Committee for UNICEF. In the Eberhard version, the old woman sells the carcass of the monster and gets rich. I have always ended by saying that she sold his hide for enough money to buy a new brass lock to keep her door shut. But bending to public opinion, I just stopped skinning the beast.

Miera Miera Meow!

A Folktale from the South of France

There once was a cat named Gattot
who lived with a sheep named Mouton.

Every day Gattot would go out to the forest to prowl.
And Mouton would busy himself around the house.

Now in the door of their snug little home,
they had a tiny cat door.
Gattot would go in and out whenever she liked.

One day when Gattot was off prowling in the forest
Monsieur Loup, the *wolf*, came to the door.
Monsieur Loup lay down
and stretched his paw through the cat door.
He began to call,
>"Mouton…
Mouton…
Come closer…
I will catch your little foot!

>Mouton…
Mouton…
Come closer…
I will catch your little tail!"

Mouton panicked!
He jumped about the house calling:
>"Gattot Gattot!
The wolf is scaring me!"

Gattot came running.
When Gattot saw the *wolf*,
her hair stood straight up.
She arched her back
and

        "Miera! Miera! *Meow*!"
And BPAOW!

She *jumped* onto that wolf's back!
        "RRROAAW!"
The wolf shook off the cat
and *ran* away fast!

Gattot went in through her little cat door.
        "Mouton, Mouton…
        you must not be frightened.
        The wolf can not get you."

        "The wolf was going to eat me up!
        The wolf was going to eat me up!"

        "Mouton…was the door locked?
        Mouton…was the window locked?
        The wolf can *not* come in the little cat door.
        The wolf can not get you.
        The wolf likes to *tease* you.
        If you do not act frightened,
        the wolf will get bored.
        Then he will go away."

Next day Gattot was off prowling in the forest.
Along came Monsieur Loup, the *wolf*.
Monsieur Loup lay down on his tummy.
He stuck his long paw through the cat door,
and he began to tease Mouton again.
        "Mouton…Mouton…Come closer…
        I'll grab your little leg!
        Mouton…Mouton…Come closer…
        I'll grab your little tail!"

Mouton began to leap around the room and cry,
        "Gattot Gattot!
        The wolf is scaring me!"

Gattot *ran* out of the forest.
When she saw the wolf,
her hair stood straight up.
She arched her back
and
        "Miera miera *meow*!"
and BPAOW!

She jumped right onto that wolf's back.
        "YARRR!"
Wolf ran off into the forest howling.

Gattot went in through her little cat door.
        "Mouton, Mouton, you must not be afraid.
        The wolf can not get you."

        "The wolf was going to eat me up!"

        "Mouton...was the door locked?
        Mouton...was the window locked?
        The wolf can *not* come through the little cat door.
        The wolf can not get you.
        Mouton, do not act frightened.
        The wolf likes to *tease* you.
        If you do not act frightened, he will go away."

Next day Gattot was off prowling in the forest.
She didn't hear Mouton calling at all.
After a while, Gattot thought she had better check.

When Gattot came near...she saw Monsieur Loup.
He was lying on his stomach.
His paw was stretched through the little cat door.
But he looked *very very* bored.
He was calling weakly,
        "Mouton...Mouton...come closer...
        I'll catch your little foot...
        Mouton...Mouton...come closer...
        I'll catch your little tail..."

And then, "KACHOO! KACHOO!" he was sneezing.
        "Stop that *Mouton*!"

And from inside the house,
Gattot heard Mouton *singing*.

> "Oh, I'm sweeping the house.
> Oh, I'm sweeping the house.
> I'm sweeping the dirt out the *cat door*!"

> "KaChoo! KaChoo!
> Stop that, *Mouton*!"

> "Well, if Mouton isn't afraid anymore,
> I don't think the wolf will bother teasing him.
> But just to make sure,
> I had better chase him off one more time."

Gattot's fur stood straight up.
She arched her back
and
> "Miera Miera *Meow*!"
and BPAOW!

She leaped straight onto Wolf's back.
> "YRAOWWW!"
Wolf shook off the cat and ran howling down the road.

Then Gattot went through her little cat door.
> "Mouton…I see you are not afraid anymore."

> "No," said Mouton.
> "The door is locked.
> The window is locked.
> And the wolf can *never* get in through that
> *tiny* cat door.
> So I am not afraid."

Since Mouton was not afraid anymore,
it was no fun at all for the wolf to tease him.
So the Monsieur Loup did not come back.

Besides, he had had enough of that
> "Miera Miera *Meow*!" and BPAOW!

Tips for telling:

I like to use the BPAOW! as a pouncing sound. I encourage the children to join me on the cat's "Miera, miera, *meow* and BPAOW!" And I prefer to use the dialectical chant "Miera, miera *meow* y BPAOW!"

About the story:

This story is elaborated from a sixteen-line tale, "Le Mouton, Le Chat et le Loup" in *Contes Populaires de L'Ariège* (Paris: Editions G.P. Maisonneuve et Larose, 1968). The tale was collected in November 1954 from Julien Blazy, a seventy-seven-year-old farmer in Lanise, Saurat region. The chant is in dialect. "*Gatot, gatot! Lé loup mé pessiga!*" "*Miéra, miéra, miaou y baou!*" Translated as: "*Petit chat, petit chat! Le loup me mord!*" "*Miéra, miéra, miaou! J'y vais!*" Clearly the dialectical chant is much more resonant than the French translation. Motif *K815.15 Cat lures young foxes from den with music. Kills them.* Our French tale is similar to Eastern European tales of susceptible characters left alone at home. MacDonald cites a Czech tale in which Budalinek is lured out by a fox; a Ukranian tale in which a cock is enticed by a fox and rescued by his partner, cat; and a Czech tale in which the child Smolichek is stolen by wood maidens and rescued by his caretaker, the stag Golden Antlers. See also Motif *J144 Well-trained kid does not open to wolf.* And note similarities to Type *123 The Wolf and the Kids.*

3 Singing Tales

FOLKTALES WITH SINGING INTERLUDES ARE COMMON IN many cultures. African and Caribbean storying uses song skillfully to involve the audience, rest the teller, and extend the story. The playful group-singing aspects are a part of the story event that everyone anticipates with pleasure.

Tales with sung refrains appear in European lore, too, and are sometimes referred to by the French term *chante fables*. And often a story moves entirely into sung format. The balladry of Great Britain and Appalachia contains many folktales shaped into song. You may want to consider incorporating a story-song or two into your storytelling events. Our use of story and song should not be a matter of one or the other. Our play should move back and forth into and out of musical expansions.

Do not think you need to have singing talent to use stories with singing interludes. It does not matter one bit what your voice sounds like. It does not even matter if you can carry a tune. If you are enthusiastic and having fun…that is all that is required. Keep in mind that the songs in these stories are all creations of the folk teller. Just as the folk story changes from teller to teller, so does the folk song. You can sing it any way you like! There is no *right* way to sing. No *correct* melody. Make the song moment into anything that pleases you and enjoy!

Several of the stories in this book make good use of singing refrains. For rousty songs see the "Drumming" and "Dancing" chapters. The two included in this "Singing Tales" chapter have especially sweet refrains.

More tales with singing refrains:

See also suggested tales in "Dancing Tales" and "Drumming Tales" sections.

"Barney McCabe" in *Ain't You Got a Right to the Tree of Life? The People of Johns Island, South Carolina—Their Faces, Their Words, and Their Songs*. Recorded and edited by Guy and Candie Carawan (Athens, Ga.: University of Georgia Press, 1989), 103–5. Great singing version of traditional tale of a boy treed by a witch and rescued by his dogs.

"The Ghost's Gold" by Heather Forest in *The Ghost and I: Scary Stories for Participatory Telling*, ed. by Jennifer Justice (Cambridge, Mass.: Yellow Moon, 1992), 50–54. Nicely adapted tale with minor-key song for ghost to wail.

"Lazy Peter" by George Shannon, in *Joining In* by Teresa Miller (Cambridge, Mass.: Yellow Moon, 1988), 89–93. A magic harmonica that makes everyone dance. George's retelling of this traditional motif allows you to insert any tune you like for the audience to join.

Lizard's Song by George Shannon, illus. by Jose Aruego and Ariane Dewey (New York: Greenwilow, 1981). Sing along with Lizard. Act it out again afterward. For another variant, see "Coyote's Crying Song" in *Twenty Tellable Tales* by Margaret Read MacDonald (New York: H.W. Wilson, 1986), 10–23.

"Rabbit and Hyena Play the Samsa" by Anne Pellowski in *The Story Vine* (New York: Macmillan, 1984), 107–10. Rabbit tricks Hyena into dancing. Pellowski suggests playing a kalimba (thumb piano) while you tell.

"Roly Poly Rice Ball" in *Twenty Tellable Tales* by Margaret Read MacDonald (New York: H.W. Wilson, 1986), 104–14. Mice sing and dance. I give children a sheet of brightly colored paper to fold a paper fan. Waving this, they sing and dance with the lady mice. We fold one end of the fan's handle under. Thus, when the fan is turned over we have a hammer to pound as we sing the men's rice pounding song.

"Snow Bunting's Lullaby" in *Tuck-Me-In Tales: Bedtime Stories from Around the World* by Margaret Read MacDonald. (Little Rock: August House, 1996). Sing along with mother bird's lullaby.

"There was an Old Woman All Skin and Bones" in *The Singing Sack* by Helen East (London: A & C Black, 1989), 45.

"There's No Such Thing" by Doug Lipman in *The Ghost and I: Scary Stories for Participatory Telling*, ed. by Jennifer Justice (Cambridge, Mass.: Yellow Moon, 1992), 41–48. Nice juxtaposition of humour and fright in this contemporary tale created by Doug Lipman.

"Trouble! (Or How the Alligator Got His Crackling Hide)" by David Holt and Bill Mooney in *Ready-to-Tell-Tales* by David Holt and Bill Mooney (Little Rock: August House, 1994), 52–56. Includes a great "trouble" song to sing along with the alligators.

Story songs:

Only a sampling of the many picture book story songs. Ask your children's librarian for more.

Fox Went Out on a Chilly Night: An Old Song written and illus. by Peter Spier (New York: Dell, 1993).

Frog Went A-Courtin' retold by John Langstaff, illus. by Feodor Rojankovsky (New York: Harcourt, Brace, 1955).

Mommy, Buy Me a China Doll, adapted from an Ozark children's song by Harve Zemach, illus. by Margot Zemach (New York: Farrar, Strauss, & Giroux, 1966).

"There Was an Old Woman All Skin and Bones" in *The Singing Sack* by Helen East (London: A & C Black, 1989), 45.

Collections with singing tales:

The Lion on the Path and Other African Stories by Hugh Tracey, illus. by Eric Byrd, music transcribed by Andrew Tracey (New York: Praeger, 1967). See "Mapandangare, the Great Baboon," "Lion on the Path," and others.

Look Back and See: Twenty Lively Tales for Gentle Tellers by Margaret Read MacDonald (New York: H.W. Wilson, 1991). "The Singing Turtle" (sing along with the many songs of turtle), "Tiny Mouse Goes Traveling" (sing Tiny Mouse's paddling song), "Kanji-jo, the Nestlings" (sing with mother bird, sing and dance with the nestlings), and others.

The Singing Sack: 28 song-stories from around the world compiled by Helen East at the National Folktale Centre, illus. by Mary Currie (London: A & C Black, 1989). Very useful collection with musical notation.

Singing Tales of Africa by Adjai Robinson, illus. by Christine Price (New York: Scribner's, 1974). See "Ayele and the Flowers," "Why There is Death in the World," and others.

Songs and Stories from Uganda by W. Moses Serwadda, transcribed and edited by Hewitt Pantaleoni, illus. by Diane and Leo Dillon (New York: Crowell, 1974). See "Nsangi" (play with audience members, accusing them of being the gorillas who ate little Nsangi, let everyone sing back with the gorillas as they deny it) and "Twerire."

Audios and Videos with Singing Tales:

Apples, Corn & Pumpkin Seeds told by The Storycrafters (Jerri Burns and Barry Marshall) (South Norwalk, Conn.: Galler West Productions, 1996), 48 min. Includes good version of "The Singing Goose." Video.

Cockroach Party! told by Margaret Read MacDonald, music by Richard Scholtz (Bellingham, Wash.: Live Music Recordings, 1999). Hear "Cockroach Party," "Pickin' Peas," "Teeny Weeny Bop," "Elk and Wren." Compact disc.

Ladder to the Moon told by The Storycrafters (Jerri Burns and Barry Marshall) (South Norwalk, Conn.: Galler West Productions, 1996), 48 min. Delightful version of "Sambalele." Video.

Mapandangare—the Great Baboon told by Andrew Tracy (Altschul Group Corp., n.d.), 10 min. Zimbabwean tale of baboon who fights off cattle thieves for girl. See this to experience the easy interface between singing, chanting teller, and chorusing audience in a traditional telling. Video.

Tell it With Me told by Doug Lipman (Albany, N.Y.: A Gentle Wind, 1985). Try "The Tailor Who Felt Wonderful," "The Magic Sausage Mill," and Doug's own creation, "Chew Your Rock Candy." Audiotape.

Tuck-Me-In Tales told by Margaret Read MacDonald, music by Richard Scholtz (Little Rock: August House, 1997). Hear "Snow Bunting's Lullaby" and "Kanji-jo, the Nestlings." Audiotape.

Bâtis! Bâtis!

A Folktale from France

There once was a little old man and a little old woman.
They had a little pet pig,
a little pet hen,
and a little pet duck.

One day the old man said to the old woman,
      "My dear, why don't we move to the forest?"

        "My dear, we don't have a house in the forest,"
          she replied.

        "My dear, we could *build* one."

        "But what about our little pig,
        and our little hen and our little duck?"

        "We could build a house for each of them too."

        "Then I'm willing to move."

So off they went…
the little old man, the little old woman,
the pig, the hen, and the duck.

They walked through valleys, they climbed over hills,
and they came to a green grassy glade.

        "This is just the spot for our houses!"

They gathered sticks…*bâtons.*
They gathered branches…*fourchettes.*
And they began to build.

"Bâtis bâtis ma petite logette.
A trois bâtons à trois fourchettes."
"Build! Build! My little house!
With three sticks and three branches!"

They built a small house for the duck.
The duck walked inside and looked around.
  "I...*like* it!"
and he shut the door.

The hen was larger,
so they built the house twice as strong for her.
  "Bâtis bâtis ma petite logette.
  A trois bâtons, à trois fourchettes.
  Bâtis bâtis ma petite logette.
  A trois bâtons, à trois fourchettes."

The hen walked inside and looked around.
  "I...*like* it!"
And she shut the door.

  "We'd better build a very strong house for the pig.
  He is *big*."

They built it three times as strong.
  "Bâtis bâtis ma petite logette.
  A trois bâtons, à trois fourchettes.
  Bâtis bâtis ma petite logette.
  A trois bâtons, à trois fourchettes.
  Bâtis bâtis ma petite logette.
  A trois bâtons, à trois fourchettes."

The pig walked inside and looked around.
  "I...*like* it!"
And he shut the door.

  "Now for a house for ourselves.
  We had better make it *very* strong.
  Let's build it *four times* stronger."

  "Bâtis bâtis ma petite logette.
  A trois bâtons, à trois fourchettes.
  Bâtis bâtis ma petite logette.
  A trois bâtons, à trois fourchettes.

Bâtis bâtis ma petite logette.
A trois bâtons, à trois fourchettes.
Bâtis bâtis ma petite logette.
A trois bâtons, à trois fourchettes."

The next morning early, early
who should come walking through the forest but…
the *wolf*!
    "What? Where did these *houses* come from?
    They weren't here *yesterday*!"
The Wolf went down to check on this.
He walked all around the little house of the duck.
    "I wonder what lives in here?"
Since it was such a flimsy house,
the wolf poked a hole through the wall
and looked inside.
    "It's a *duck*!
    I like duck!"
Then the wolf began to call:
    "Little duck…
    little duck…
    What are you doing in there?"

Inside the duck was having his breakfast.
    "I'm nibbling.
    I'm nibbling.
    I'm nibbling up my breakfast."

    "Open the door, little duck.
    I'll come in and nibble with you."

But the Duck could recognize that voice.
    "I'm not *stupid*.
    You sound like the *wolf*.
    You'd eat me up."

    "If you don't open the door,
    I'll make such a wind.
    I will *blow* your door down."

So the wolf began to blow.
    "Petay! Petay! Petay!"
He blew down the door and ate up the duck.

"Now whose house is *this*?"
The wolf poked a little hole through the hen's house
and peeked inside.

"It's a *hen*!
I like hen!
Little hen…
little hen…
what are you doing in there?"

"I'm pecking.
I'm pecking.
I'm pecking up my breakfast."

"Open the door
and I'll come in and peck with you."

"I'm not *stupid*!
You sound like the *wolf*!
You'd eat me up."

"If you don't open the door,
I'll make such a wind.
I will blow your door down."

And he began to blow.
"*Petay! Petay! Petay!*"
He blew down the door and ate up the hen.

"Now look at this *big* house.
I wonder who lives here."

The wolf tried to poke a hole in little pig's house.
But that house had been built three times as strong.
He could not poke a hole into *that* house.

"Who lives in the little house?
Who is inside?"

"Grunt. Grunt. It's *me*. The *pig*."

"Little pig…
little pig…
what are you doing in there?"

"I'm gobbling.
I'm gobbling.
I'm gobbling up my breakfast."

"Open the door
and I will come in and gobble with you."

"I'm not *stupid*!
You sound like the *wolf*!
You'd eat me up."

"Then I will make such a wind
that I will blow your door down."

And the wolf began to blow.
      "*Petay! Petay! Petay!*"
But the pig's house was strong.
      "*Petay! Petay! Petay!*"
The wolf could not blow the pig's door down.

So the wolf tried another plan.
      "Little pig, do you like potatoes?"

      "I *love* potatoes."

      "I know where there is a fine potato patch.
      I'll take you there tomorrow morning."

      "Where is the potato patch?"

      "Down the hill and to the left."

      "What time will you come?"

      "6 A.M."

      "See you then."

The little pig got up the next morning at 5 A.M.
He went down the hill and to the left
and dug a whole sack of potatoes.
Then he took them home, went inside,
locked the door, and cooked potatoes!

At 6 A.M., the wolf arrived.
"Little pig...let's go dig potatoes."

"I'm eating.
I'm eating.
I'm already *eating* potatoes."

The wolf was annoyed.
"Well...little pig...
Do you like apples?"

"I *love* apples."

"Would you go with me tomorrow morning to pick
apples?"

"I'll go. Where is the apple tree?"

"Down the hill and to the right.
See you at 6."

Next morning the little pig got up at 5 A.M.
and went down the hill and to the right.
He climbed up the tree with his big copper bucket
and began to fill it with apples.

But the wolf was not stupid either.
At 5:30, here came the wolf.

"Little pig...
little pig...
what are you doing up there?"

"I'm picking.
I'm picking.
I'm picking all the apples."

"Little pig, jump down with an apple for me."

"Just open your mouth and I'll *throw* one down."
So the wolf opened his mouth,
and the little pig threw down an apple.

"Little pig, jump down with an apple for me."

"Just open your mouth and I'll *throw* another down."
The wolf opened his mouth
and the pig threw another apple.

"Little pig, jump down
with a whole bucketful of apples for me!"

"Okay wolf. Get ready! I am going to jump."

The wolf held his mouth wide, wide open,
ready to catch that little pig in his jaws.

But the pig lifted his heavy copper bucket *full* of apples
and dropped it into the wolf's gullet.
WHUNK!
The poor wolf was knocked silly from the blow.
And before he could come to,
the little pig had taken an apple for himself,
an apple for the little old woman,
and an apple for the little old man,
and run along home.

"I doubt the wolf will come again," he told them.
"He has had a taste of *pig*,
and that should cure his hunger for a while.
But just to be sure,
we had better build strong *strong* houses
for our next little duck and little hen."
So they set to work
and built a house for a hen and a house for a duck.
Very strong houses.

"*Bâtis bâtis ma petite logette.*
A trois bâtons, à trois fourchettes.
Bâtis bâtis ma petite logette.
A trois bâtons, à trois fourchettes.
Bâtis bâtis ma petite logette.
A trois bâtons, à trois fourchettes.
Bâtis bâtis ma petite logette.
A trois bâtons, à trois fourchettes."

So that wolf could *never* break them down again.

Tips for telling:

I sing the *"Bâtis, bâtis"* chant to the tune below and we make building motions as if piling stick onto stick as we sing. Children sometimes also join in with the hen and pig as they survey their house and state "I...*like* it!" This is, of course, fun to act out with a little old man, a little old woman, and a few ducks, hens, pigs, and wolves. If you just can't stand to have the duck and hen eaten up permanently, you have a chance to cut them out while the wolf is lying in a stupor under the apple tree. Then sew him up and run away quick.

Bâtis, bâtis!

Bâ - tis, bâ - tis ma pe - tite lo - gette, à trois bâ - tons, à trois four - chettes.

About the story:

Retold from "Le Loup et le Goret" in *Contes de L'Ouest* by Geneviève Massignon (Paris: Editions Erasme, 1954), 187–91. The story was told by Mme Vve Honoré Gibault of L'Ille d'Elle (Vendée) in 1950. She was seventy-eight years old. I have changed the French "péter" to "petay" for the wolf's blowing. The French wolf blew the door down in a somewhat impolite way! This is Aarne-Thompson Type *124 Blowing the House in. The goose builds a house of feathers; the hog one of stone. The wolf blows the goose's house in and eats her. Cannot blow down the hog's house. Finally he is allowed to enter. He is tricked into the chimney (or churn) where he is burned up.* Also Motif *Z81 Blowing the house in* and Motif *K864 Fatal apple-throwing game.*

Telesik

A Folktale from the Ukraine

When Telesik was little
he begged and begged his parents
to give him a little boat of his own
so he could go out on the lake and fish.

At last his father made him a little golden boat
and a little silver oar.
      "You may go out on the lake alone, little Telesik,"
said his Momma.
      "But do not come to the shore,
      unless you hear your Momma calling.
      If a stranger calls to you…
      row past and away."

Every day Telesik would row out
into the middle of the lake.

He would lower his line and wait…
…caught one!

He would lower his line and wait…
…caught one!

At lunchtime Telesik's Momma would come to the shore.
She would call to him.
      "Telesik…Telesik…
      Come to your Momma…
      Telesik…Telesik…
      Come to your Momma…"

Then Telesik would sing to his boat.
      "Row Golden Boat,
      Row Silver Oar.

Carry Little Telesik
        Closer to the shore."
And his boat would skim over the water
and bring him to where his Momma was waiting.

She would hand him a little jug of tea
and a little basket of goodies for his lunch.

Then he would sing.
        "Row Golden Boat.
        Row Silver Oar.
        Carry Little Telesik
        Away from the shore."
His boat would sail back to the middle of the lake,
and Telesik would eat his lunch.

One day when Telesik's mother was calling,
a nasty Dragon lady was passing by.
She heard Telesik's mother call,
and she saw his boat sail to the shore.

        "That Telesik would make a tasty supper,"
thought the Dragon.
        I will call him to the shore and *catch* him."

So she went down to the shore
and hid herself in the rushes.
Then she called, in her husky dragon voice,
        "Telesik…
        Telesik…
        Come to your Momma!

        Telesik…
        Telesik…
        Come to your Momma!"

When Telesik heard that he cried,
        "That's a *scratchy* voice.
        That can't be my Momma."

And he sang out:
        "Row Golden Boat.
        Row Silver Oar.

Carry Little Telesik
away from the shore!"

So the Dragon couldn't catch him after all.
"There is something wrong with my voice,"
thought the Dragon.
"I'll have to find out how his mother sings."

Next day when Telesik's Momma came down to the shore,
the Dragon was hiding to listen.
"Telesik…Telesik…
Come to your Momma!
Telesik…Telesik…
Come to your Momma!"

"*That* is my mother's voice," said Telesik.
"She sings high and sweet."

"Row Golden Boat.
Row Silver Oar.
Carry Little Telesik
Closer to the shore."
His little boat skimmed over the water
and Telesik got his lunch.

But the Dragon went away and began practicing.
"'Telesik…'
Too scratchy.
'Telesik…'
Too scratchy.
'Telesik…'
That's better.
'Telesik…'
Make it higher.
'Telesik…'
Make it sweeter.
'Telesik…Telesik…
Come to your Momma!'
Just *right*!

So next day when Telesik was out fishing,
the Dragon hurried down to the lake
before his mother arrived.

She hid herself in the rushes and called…
      "Telesik…
      Telesik…
      Come to your Momma!"

      "Mother has come early today," thought Telesik.
And he sang:
      "Row Golden Boat
      Row Silver Oar.
      Carry Little Telesik
      Closer to the shore."

When he had skimmed right up to the shore,
the Dragon stuck her long arm out and called…
      "Telesik…Telesik…
      Come a little closer.
      Telesik…Telesik…
      Just a little closer.
      Telesik…Telesik…
      I've GOT YOU!"

And throwing him into her sack,
she carried him off through the fields to her home.

But Telesik was too heavy to carry so far.
After a while the Dragon stopped to rest.
      "Here Telesik," she said.
      "Stay quiet in the bag while I nap."

As soon as the Dragon was sleeping soundly,
Telesik wiggled out of the bag,
ran to a nearby sycamore tree,
and climbed to the top to hide.

When the Dragon awakened she picked up her bag.
      "What's this?
      My Little Telesik has escaped, has he?
      Well I'll soon find him again."

Snuffling along…she followed his trail…
straight to the sycamore tree.
      "You think you can escape from me so easily?
      I will chop down the tree with my sharp sharp teeth.

It will take me awhile.
But I'll *do* it."
The Dragon began to gnaw and gnaw
on the trunk of that sycamore tree.

In the top of the tree, Little Telesik was frightened.
But just then he saw a flock of geese.
They were flying south for the winter.
"Geese! Geese!
Fly down quick!
Rescue Little Telesik!"

But the geese called,
"HONK—HONK…HONK—HONK—HONK…
We can't be bothered…
HONK—HONK…HONK—HONK—HONK…
Let the geese behind us rescue you."
And they flew on.

The Dragon was gnawing away.
"This tree is harder than I thought.
But I will gnaw it through!"

Another formation of geese flew over.
"Geese! Geese!
Fly down quick!
Rescue Little Telesik!"

"HONK—HONK…HONK—HONK—HONK…
We can't be bothered.
HONK—HONK…HONK—HONK—HONK…
Let the geese behind us rescue you."
And they flew on.

The Dragon had almost gnawed through the sycamore tree.

Here came another flock of geese.
"Geese! Geese!
Fly down quick!
Rescue Little Telesik!"

"HONK—HONK…HONK—HONK—HONK…
We can't be bothered

HONK—HONK…HONK—HONK—HONK…
    Let the geese behind us rescue you."
And they flew on.

The Dragon had nearly gnawed through the sycamore.
The huge tree was starting to wobble…
back and forth…

Here was one last little goose flying all alone.
She had been left behind by her family
and was trying so hard to catch up.
        "Goose! Goose!
        Come down quick!
        Rescue Little Telesik!"

And then he added…
        "You *have* to rescue me.
        You are my last chance!"

The little goose came down.
She took Telesik on her back
and flew right back to his house.

His mother came out…
        "Oh Telesik! We were so worried.
        Your boat was empty.
        And *look*…you brought home a goose for our dinner!"

        "No! No!" said Telesik.
        "This goose saved my life!
        You cannot eat *it*!"

So the little goose stayed the winter with Telesik.
They fed her and took good care of her.
And in the spring when her family returned,
she flew off north with them again.

As for the Dragon…
why, she never came back in that neighborhood again.
I hear she ruined her teeth
gnawing on that hard, hard sycamore tree.

Tips for telling:

I encourage the children to sing and row with me as Telesik rows to shore. I sing it as a gentle, rocking-on-the-water type of song. Sometimes the audience also will join in on the mother's call. I accept this participation but do not solicit it.

Telesik's Song

Row, gold - en boat, row, sil - ver oar.

Car - ry lit - tle Tel - e - sik clos - er to the shore.

Telesik's Mother's Song

Tel - e - sik, Tel - e - sik, come to your mom - ma!

After the story is told, I pass out squares of paper in a blue shade, and we fold a paper boat while talking about the story. We make a fold, then use our origami shape to re-enact a bit of the story and sing. This gives us a break from the intensity of trying to figure out creases and allows any stragglers to catch up in their folding. If there are a few parents in the audience to help with the youngest children, this works fine for family storytimes. We take our time with the exercise and I move around helping anyone who is having trouble.

Instructions

Start with: 1 piece of typing paper cut to 8½ x 8½. I like to use a shade of blue.

1. Fold paper in center. Crease.
2. Open. Fold paper to center from the other direction. Crease.
3. Open paper. Fold from each side to the center crease. (the only reason you folded in the center was to make a mark for the children to line up this fold). Crease the two edges.

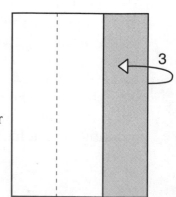

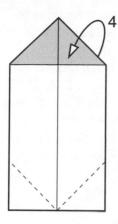 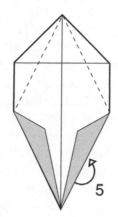 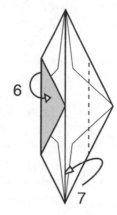

4. Fold each corner up, lining it's side up with the interior crease. Float it around in the air and sing Telesik's boat song.

5. Starting at the center fold and reaching to the boat's point, make a long triangular fold. Repeat this on all four corners. Say, "Remember how the geese flew by?" Imitate the geese flying with your winged origami. Fly it in the air and honk, "HONK—HONK…HONK—HONK—HONK…We can't carry you. Let the geese behind us carry you."

6. Fold each side point over to the middle opening. Sing your flying goose song again, and fly your origami around.

7. Put your thumbs inside the opening and open. You have a boat shape. Hold it up and sing "Row Golden Boat, Row Silver Oar. Carry Little Telesik closer to the shore."

8. Now, holding your thumbs inside, turn the boat inside out. You now have a sturdy little boat. Hold the boat in the air and sing two or three choruses of Telesik's boat song.

About the story:

This story is inspired by "Telesik-Little Stick" in *Ukranian Folk Tales*, translated by Irina Zheleznova (Kieve: Dnipro Publishers, 1981), 96–102. I have omitted the beginning sequence of this story in which an old man and old woman wish for a child and put a stick in a cradle. The stick turns to a child. He is called "Telesik-Little Stick." The ogress in the Zheleznova version is a snake. When Telesik is captured he is taken to her home and given to Olenka, the snake daughter, to cook. He tricks her into the oven and escapes, then calls down from the tree telling the snake that she ate her daughter. The illustration shows Telesik putting a little girl into the oven (not an actual snake). Since I wanted to use Telesik with very young children I left out the poking the daughter in the fire motif. I tried calling the ogress a "Snake-Lady" or a "Snake-Ogress," but this didn't seem quite right, so I finally decided to just call her a Dragon. After all, a large snake that eats up little boys is pretty much a Dragon, and the imagery works better. In variants cited below the ogre is sometimes a witch, sometimes a dragon.

This is Type *327F The Witch and the Fisher Boy. Witch has her tongue made thin by blacksmith so as to change her voice [F556.2, K1832]. She thus entices the fisher boy [G413].* Aarne-Thompson cite variants from Russia, the Ukraine, Bulgaria, and Lithuania. This story also includes Type *327C The Devil (Witch) Carries the Hero Home in a Sack. The wife or daughter are to cook him but are thrown into the oven themselves.* Motifs include: *K1832 Disguise by changing voice; G413 Ogre disguises voice to lure victims; B542.1 Bird flies with man to safety;* and *R251 Flight on tree which ogre tries to cut down.* MacDonald's *Storyteller's Sourcebook* gives three variants under R251: *Ivanko and the Dragon: an Old Ukrainian Folk Tale* from the Original Collection of Ivan Rudchenko (New York: Atheneum, 1969) [ogre is a dragon, swans carry]; *Ivan and the Witch: A Russian Tale* by Mischa Damjan (New York: McGraw-Hill, 1969) [ogre is witch]; and "Ivanko and the Witch" in *Russian Tales of Fabulous Beasts and Marvels* by Lee Wyndham (New York: Parent's, 1969), 32–41. Compare also to the Norwegian story "Little Buttercup" in *When the Lights Go Out* by Margaret Read MacDonald (New York: H.W. Wilson, 1988), 7–20, in which a boy is carried off by a witch, escapes her bag, burns up her husband and daughter, and climbs her chimney.

4 Dancing Tales

SOME OF MY FAVORITE TALES ARE DANCING TALES. AND OF course…you don't have to know how to dance. You just have to have joy in your soul. Our society is so lacking in opportunities for children and adults to sing, dance, and use their bodies and voices freely. Share some dancing tales and let your audience party! Any way they want to move to the rhythm of your song is just the *right* way.

"El Conejito" is an especially useful vehicle for enticing audiences to dance. In "El Conejito" we first learn Conejito's song. Then, during the story, the audience sings and claps each time Conejito dances. By the time we reach the story's finale, they are ready to jump up and dance *with* Conejito. I encourage more and more body movement by asking them to sing of Tia's dancing skirt while shaking imaginary skirts, then move to dancing arms, dancing feet, and finally dancing hips! By this time even the most timid are loosening up.

To encourage freedom of movement among the children with whom you work, you might want to make dancing activities a regular part of your classroom or library life. For this I particularly like the song "Tingalayo" as performed by Parachute Express on *Shakin' It* (Burbank: Walt Disney Records, 1992). I begin by letting the children trot in a circle to the "run little donkey run" refrain. Then, at certain spots in the music, we stop and just shake our hips and dance. It is fun to play rhythm sticks to this tune too. Repeat the same song over several days and see the children begin to move more freely to the music. On the Parachute Express CD this song is followed by a quiet piece, "Who will draw a ring around the moon?" I motion for the children to sit down quietly, and we use large, slow arm movements to draw a ring around the moon as we listen to this piece. It is important to include such peaceful moments in your day's activities, as well as the boisterous play promoted in this book.

While the stories suggested in this chapter all include dancing, I usually do not get the audience onto their feet for a free-for-all dance until the end of the story. Exceptions are the two Diane Wolkstein stories listed below. In those stories, I bring the audience to their feet during the telling. For another story in which I get the audience up during the story, see "Poule and Roach," which is listed in the drumming chapter. In that story, I have the audience on their feet doing exercises several times! Getting the entire audience to their feet during a story is risky. It upsets them and breaks their listening track. But it also gives them a stretch!

Here is a list of tales that might inspire dancing, and texts for two of my favorite dancing tales. For other tales that include dancing see references for "Kanji-jo, the Nestlings" (p. 33), "Roly Poly Rice Ball" (p. 32), "Mabela the Clever" (p. 114), and "Turtle of Koka" (p. 84). See also all stories in the chapter on "Drumming Tales."

Stories to dance:

Abiyoyo: based on a South African Lullaby and Folk Story by Pete Seeger, illus. by Michael Hays (New York: Simon & Schuster, 1986). Help sing to make the monster dance. Get up at the end and dance with it.

Dance Away by George Shannon, illus. Jose Aruego and Ariane Dewey (New York: Greenwillow, 1982). Lead audience in dancing while seated during story. Get up and act it out and dance it at the end.

"The Horned Animals' Party" by Diane Ferlatte in *Ready-to-Tell Tales* by David Holt and Bill Mooney (Little Rock: August House, 1994), 101–4. Lots of action as the animals dance. Get the audience up onto their feet at the end and let everyone join in the party.

"Horse and Toad" in *The Magic Orange Tree and Other Tales from Haiti* by Diane Wolkstein (New York: Knopf, 1978), 143–50. Toad and Horse race. Each must sing his song at every milepost. The audience sings Horse's song with me. I ask them all to stand up each time and sway back and forth as horse sings.

"Papa God and the Pintards" in *Celebrate the World* by Margaret Read MacDonald (New York: H.W. Wilson, 1994), 193–97. The guinea fowls make Papa God dance. Be sure your audience jumps up to dance with them at the end.

"A Penny and a Half," described on page 114, ends with the animals dancing. It could be fun to add a song to the ending and let everyone dance around the room for a while.

"Uncle Bouki Dances the Kokioko" in *The Magic Orange Tree and Other Tales from Haiti* by Diane Wolkstein (New York: Knopf, 1978), 79–86. The King of Haiti invents a dance and offers a prize for anyone who can perform it. Heavyset Uncle Bouki practices and wins the prize. This is another great story for getting your audience up and dancing. I begin by asking my audience to join the King of Haiti in the arm motions for his dance. By the time Uncle Bouki is ready to perform at the palace, everyone has the arm motions down and is ready to jump up and *dance*. I insist that *everyone* in the room dance along…even the teachers in the back. Then I toss them all imaginary prize money as a reward for finishing the dance.

El Conejito
A Folktale from Panama

Había una vez un conejito
que vivía muy contento con su mamá.

Once upon a time there was a little rabbit
who lived so happily with his mama.

One day Conejito's Mamá said,
> "Conejito, it is summer vacation!
> You can go up the mountain to visit your Tía Monica.
> Auntie Monica is going to feed you cakes...
> and candies...and cookies...
> and every good thing...
> until you are fat as a...*butterball*!"

Conejito was so happy.
> "I *love* to visit my Tía Monica!"
So Conejito went dancing up the mountain
...*bailando y saltando.*

He was singing about his Tía Monica!
Tía Monica loved to eat *and* she loved to dance!
> "I have a sweet old Auntie.
> My Tía Monica!
> And when she goes out dancing...
> They all say, 'Oooh la la!'"

Running along and singing,
he didn't look where he was going and...
WHUNK!
He ran right into...*Señor Zorro!*
Señor Fox!
> "Conejito! Conejito!" said Señor Zorro.
> "I think I have just met my...*lunch*!"

"No! No! No!" cried Conejito.
"You don't want *me* for lunch!
Just *look* at me how *skinny* I am.
Flaquito! Flaquito! Flaquito!
(Skinny! Skinny! Skinny!)
Wait until I come back from my Tía Monica's house.
Auntie Monica is going to feed me cakes…
and candies…and cookies…
and every good thing.
Until I am fat as a…*butterball!*"

"Mmmm," said Señor Zorro.
"I *like* the sound of that.
I'll eat you when you come back."

So Conejito went on up the mountain…
bailando y saltando.
    "I have a sweet old Auntie.
    My Tía Monica!
    And when she goes out dancing…
    They all say, 'Oooh la la!'"

And running along and singing,
he ran right into…WHUNK!
Señor Tigre!
Señor Tiger!
    "Conejito! Conejito!
    I think I have just met my…*lunch!*"

    "No! No! No!" cried Conejito.
    "You don't want *me* for lunch!
    Just *look* at me.
    Flaquito! Flaquito! Flaquito!
    Wait until I come back from my Tía Monica's house.
    Auntie Monica is going to feed me cakes…
    and candies…and cookies…
    and every good thing.
    Until I am fat as a…*butterball!*"

    "Mmmm," said Señor Tigre.
    "I *like* the sound of that.
    I'll eat you when you come back."

So Conejito went on up the mountain...
bailando y saltando.
> "I have a sweet old Auntie.
> My Tía Monica!
> And when she goes out dancing...
> They all say, 'Oooh la la!'"

And running along and singing,
he ran right into...WHUNK!
Señor León!
Señor Lion!
> "Conejito! Conejito!
> I think I have just met my...*lunch*!"

> "No! No! No!" cried Conejito.
> "You don't want *me* for lunch!
> Just *look* at me.
> *Flaquito! Flaquito! Flaquito!*
> Wait until I come back from my Tía Monica's house.
> Auntie Monica is going to feed me cakes...
> and candies...and cookies...
> and every good thing.
> Until I am fat as a...*butterball*!"

> "Mmmm," said Señor León.
> "I *like* the sound of that.
> I'll eat you when you come back."

So Conejito went on up the mountain...
bailando y saltando.
> "I have a sweet old Auntie.
> My Tía Monica!
> And when she goes out dancing...
> They all say, 'Oooh la la!'"

And running along and singing,
he ran right into...WHUNK!
Tía Monica!
> "Conejito! Conejito!" said Tía Monica.
> "Have you come to visit?
> Do you want me to feed you cakes...
> and candies...and cookies...
> and every good thing?"

"Yes please, Auntie!"
So his Tía Monica feed Conejito cakes…
and candies…
and cookies…
and every good thing.
Until he was fat as a…*butterball*!

But she also fed him fresh fruits and vegetables
and good mountain water
so he would be strong and healthy.

And then it was time to go back home again.

"Tía Monica, I am afraid to go back down the
    mountain," said Conejito.
On the mountain I met a fox and a tiger and a lion.
And they are all waiting to *eat me up*!"

"Oh we can fool them," said Tía Monica.
And she brought out a large barrel.

"Just pop inside, Conejito.
And you can roll right down the mountain.
Roll right past Señor León.
Roll right past Señor Tigre.
Roll right past Señor Zorro.
And roll right to your Mamá's house!"

Then Tía Monica had another idea.
"I am going to build a big smoky fire in my yard,"
    she said.
"You must tell those nasty fellows that
the mountain is on fire!
Then we'll see them *run*!"

So Conejito climbed inside the barrel.
His Auntie put on the lid.
Then she gave the barrel a little push…
Down the mountainside he rolled…
rodando…rodando…rodando…
rodando…rodando…rodando…
right into Señor León…WHUNK!

"*Barrilito*! *Barrilito*!
Have you seen Conejito?
Little barrel, little barrel.
Have you seen Conejito?"

From inside the barrel, Conejito called out.
"The mountain's on fire!
Conejito is too!
Run quick, Señor Lion!
Or you'll be *barbecue*!"

Señor León looked up.
There was smoke on the mountaintop.
"The mountain's on fire!
I'll be *barbecue*!"
He ran out of there *so fast*.

On down the hill rolled Conejito in his barrel.
*Rodando…rodando…rodundo…
rodando…rodando…rodando…*
right into Señor Tigre…WHUNK!

"*Barrilito*! *Barrilito*!
Have you seen Conejito?"

From inside the barrel, Conejito called out.
"The mountain's on fire!
Conejito is too!
Run quick, Señor Tigre!
Or you'll be *barbecue*!"

Señor Tigre looked up.
Smoke on the mountaintop!
"The mountain's on fire!
I'll be *barbecue*!"
He ran out of there *so fast*.

On down the hill rolled Conejito in his barrel.
*Rodando…rodando…rodando…
rodando…rodando…rodando…*
right into Señor Zorro…WHUNK!

"*Barrilito*! *Barrilito*!
Have you seen Conejito?"

From inside the barrel, Conejito called out.
"The mountain's on fire!
Conejito is too!
Run quick, Señor Zorro!
Or you'll be *barbecue*!"

Señor Zorro looked up.
Smoke on the mountaintop!
"The mountain's on fire!
I'll be *barbecue*!"
He ran out of there *so fast*.

And Conejito rolled on down the mountain.
Rodando...rodando...rodando...
Rodando...rodando...rodando...
...WHUNK!

Right into his own Mamá.

"*Barrilito*! *Barrilito*!
Have you seen Conejito?"

And from inside the barrel Conejito called out,
"Mamá, it's *me*!"
She took off the lid and lifted him out.
My, but he was fat as a...*butterball*!

"Conejito! Conejito!
Our Tía Monica really *did* feed you well!
Good old Tía Monica!"

And so they danced and sang Auntie Monica's song.
"We have a sweet old Auntie!
Our Tía Monica!
And when she goes out dancing...
They all say, 'Oooh la la!'

And so her feet are dancing,
her feet are dancing so.
And so her feet are dancing.
Her feet are dancing so.

And so her arms are dancing,
her arms are dancing so.
And so her arms are dancing.
Her arms are dancing so.

And so her hips are dancing.
Her hips are dancing so.
And so her hips are dancing.
Her hips are dancing so.

We have a sweet old Auntie.
Our Tía Monica.
And when she goes out dancing.
They all say, 'Ooh la la!'"

Tips for telling:

Use as much or as little of the Spanish language as feels comfortable.
The actual chant in the Panamanian tale is:
"La montaña está prendida,
el conejito se quemó;
sal huyendo león,
que te vuelves chicharrón."

Conejito's dancing song in Spanish is:
"Tenemos una Tía
La Tía Monicá!
Y cuando va de comprear,
decimos, 'Ooh la la!'"

"Asi baila la falda
La falda baile asi.
Asi baila la falda
La falda baile asi."

The song can go on as long as you wish, singing about tia's scarf,
blouse, shoes, handbag. It is of course sung with dancing and swishing
of pretend skirts, twirling of pretend handbags and scarves. I have
changed the text of the chorus from "when she goes out shopping" to
"when she goes out dancing." And I find it easier to get young children
dancing if I sing of their feet, arms, etc., dancing, rather than imaginary clothing. Repeat the chorus between each verse.

Encourage the audience to sing Conejito's song with you from the
beginning. With some audiences, it works best to teach them the song
before you begin by singing it through a time or two. Usually I just
start into the story and take time at the song's first instance to repeat
it until the audience is singing along. They can be encouraged to clap,

too. Be sure to get them up to sing *and* dance the entire song at the tale's end. By having them dancing with their feet, hands, hips, you can gradually get them shaking it up! Don't stop until you get some *action* out of those little bodies.

Jen and Nat Whitman found this a great tandem piece. Jen tells the story, acts Conejito's part, and exhorts the audience to sing along. Nat lurks about as the various villains, and appears as Tía Monica and Mamá. It also makes a great act-it-out story for your whole group. Assign a few kids to play León, Zorro, Tigre, Mamá, and Tía Monica. Everyone else is a Conejito. You retell the story leading your gang of rabbits about from villain to villain. We had great fun with this at Northwest Teacher Camp dancing through the meadow while lions, tigers, and foxes lurked behind trees ready to pounce. If you could find a grassy slope it would be fun to actually lie down and roll *rodando…rodando…rodando…*

Conejito's Song

I had a sweet old aunt-ie my Aunt-ie Mon-i-ca, and when she goes out dan-cing they all say Ooh-La-La!

About the story:

This story is retold from "El Conejito" in the collection *El Conejito: Narrativa Oral Panameña* by Rogelio Sinán, illustrated by Jorge Korea (Editorial Universitaria Centroamericana), 7–14. I have introduced into the story a dancing song that I learned at a Girl Scout camp in Puerto Rico in 1963. I had help in shaping this story from the tandem performances of Jen and Nat Whitman (The Whitman Story Sampler).

Another Panamian variant appears in *The Enchanted Orchard and Other Folktales of Central America* by Dorothy Sharp Carter (Harcourt, Brace, Jovanovich, 1972), 87–90. MacDonald cites several similar tales under *K553.0.3* "I'll be fatter when I return."* In an Indian version Lambikin rolls in a drum past jackal, vulture, and tiger en route to Grandma's house. Nepali and Indian versions feature an old woman in a rolling pumpkin. For an Iranian version of the old woman in a pumpkin tale see "The Old Woman in a Pumpkin Shell" in MacDonald's *Celebrate the World* (New York: H.W. Wilson, 1994), 61–70.

Pickin' Peas

A Folktale from Alabama

Retold from the picture book *Pickin' Peas* by Margaret Read MacDonald,
illustrated by Pat Cummins. With permission of HarperCollins Publishers.

In the springtime
Little Girl planted a garden full of peas.
Come July those peas got ripe and ready to eat.
Little Girl started going down the row,
pickin' those peas.
Singing:

> "Pickin' peas.
> Put 'em in my pail.
> Pickin' peas.
> Put 'em in my pail."

She was just picking off the biggest ones.
Left the little bitty ones to grow some more.

A pesky rabbit lived down in the holler behind her house.
He jumped in the row behind her.
Started hopping along eating her peas.
Singing:

> "Pickin' peas.
> Land on my knees!
> Pickin' peas.
> Land on my knees!"

Every time he'd sing, he'd give a little jump.
And he'd land on his knees every time.

He came down that row eating up all the peas she'd left behind.

> "Pickin' peas.
> Land on my knees!
> Pickin' peas.
> Land on my knees!"

Mr. Rabbit was moving along just one row behind Little Girl.
When she'd turn the corner at the east end of the garden,
and start *down* a row,
he'd turn the corner at the west end of the garden,
and start *up* a row.

> "Pickin' peas.
> Put 'em in my pail."
> > "Pickin' peas.
> > Land on my knees!"
>
> "Pickin' peas.
> Put 'em in my pail!"
> > "Pickin' peas.
> > Land on my knees!"

After a while Little Girl got to feeling like somebody was following
    her.
Said to herself,

> "I think I'll cut my song off short
> and see what I hear."

She sang:

> "Pickin' peas.
> Put 'em in my pail.
> Pickin' peas.
> Put 'em in my..."

Listened. Heard.

> "...Land on my knees."

Little Girl said, "*Aha*!

> I do believe that pesky rabbit is in my garden.
> I do believe he's following me.
> I do believe he's pickin' my *peas*!"

She thought a minute.

> "I do believe,
> if I turn back around the end of this row,
> I can *catch* him!"

Little Girl started tiptoeing back up the row she'd already picked.

> "Pickin' peas.
> Put 'em in my pail..."

There was Mr. Rabbit hopping along down at the end of that row.

> "Pickin' peas.
> Land on my knees!"

She crept up behind him real quiet.
     "Pickin' peas.
     Land on my knees!"
She reached out…
     "Pickin' peas.
     Land on my…WHOAPP!"
She *caught him*.

Said "Mr. Rabbit.
     What's that you were singing just now?"

Mr. Rabbit scrunched up.
Said, "Ooooohhhh…I was singing…
     "Diggin' up roots.
     Land on my foots."

     "That's not what you were singing!"
She squeezed him harder.
     "What were you singing?"

     "Ooooohhhh…" in a squinchy little voice.
     "I was singing,
     Pickin' peas,
     Land on my knees!"

     "That's what I *thought* you were singing,"
said Little Girl.
     "You were eating up my *peas* weren't you?"

     " Mmmmm, maybe."

     "Well, you won't pick *my* peas anymore.
     I'm going to take you home.
     I'm going to put you in a box.
     I'm going to keep you there
     till the pea-picking season is *over*."

She took that rabbit home.
Put him in a box.
Shut the lid down real tight.
Cooked a mess of peas.
And ate them all up.

"Well, *that* was good."
Little Girl heard Mr. Rabbit hopping around inside that box.
He was singing.

> "Pickin' peas.
> Land on my knees!
> Pickin' peas.
> Land on my knees!
> Heard my momma calling me
> right over there!"

> "Mr. Rabbit, what's that you're doing in there?"

> "Trying to dance, but it's too crowded in here.
> Take me out and put me up on top of the box.
> I'll dance and entertain you."

> "Let me see that."

She took him out and put him up on top of the box.
He began to dance and sing.

> "Pickin' peas.
> Land on my knees!
> Pickin' peas.
> Land on my knees!
> Heard my momma callin' me
> *right* over there."

Every time he sang "*right* over there,"
he gave a little jump to the right.

> "That's *good* dancing!" said Little Girl.

> "Put me up on that big chest by the window,
> and I could dance even *better*," said Mr. Rabbit.

Little Girl put him up on the big chest by the window.
Mr. Rabbit started really cutting up.

> "Pickin' peas.
> Land on my knees!
> Pickin' peas.
> Land on my knees.
> Heard my momma callin' me
> *right* over there!"

Little Girl was clapping and laughing.
>"I *love* your dancing, Mr. Rabbit."

>"Put me up on that windowsill,
>and I could *really* dance!" said Mr. Rabbit.

So Little Girl picked him up.
Set him down on that broad windowsill by the open window.
Mr. Rabbit was jumping up and down, kicking his heels.
>"Pickin' peas.
>Land on my knees.
>Pickin' peas.
>Land on my knees.
>Heard my momma callin' me
>*right* over there."

...and *out* the window he went.

Mr. Rabbit ran off through the garden calling.
>"Picked your peas.
>And I landed on my knees.
>Gonna eat all I want
>'Cause you can't catch me!"

I'd like to say that's the last Little Girl saw of that rabbit.
But I'm afraid he was right back there the next morning.
>Pickin' peas...
>and landin' on his *knees*!

Tips for telling:

Encourage your audience to sing along with you. I ask them to make the motion of picking peas and dropping them in a pail while Little Girl sings. We slap our legs in a landing motion as Mr. Rabbit hops. If my audience is participating well, I sometimes divide them into Girls and Rabbits and let each side of the audience sing their own song. This story is easy to act out. Divide your group into teams and let them act it as a tandem story play. Or divide the whole group into a batch of rabbits and a batch of little girls and jump and pick as you act it out. With preschoolers I use the latter technique. I simply retell the story as we recreate it in movement. It is fun to let everyone really cut up and dance with Mr. Rabbit in the second part of the story.

Pickin' Peas

About the story:

This story appears, in slightly different telling, in the picture book *Pickin' Peas* by Margaret Read MacDonald, illustrated by Pat Cummings (New York: HarperCollins, 1998). Used with permission of HarperCollins Publishers. The story was collected in Calhoun, Alabama, and published in *Southern Workman,* Vol. 26, No. 12 (December 1897). A version told by Sarah Demings from Elizabeth City County, Virginia, was published in the *Journal of American Folklore*, Vol. 35 (1922), 273–74. Motif *K606 Escape by singing songs.*

5 Drumming Tales

AND NOW FOR SOMETHING COMPLETELY WILD. STORIES that include drumming can be great fun. But they *can* get away from you if you are not careful. If you are unsure of your ability to control your group, you can minimize the damage by asking them to drum with two fingers on their desktops or on a book. This produces a pleasing rhythmical effect and does *not* bring the principal running. And if a few drummers go berserk, the effect is still not so bad.

Drums can be made by covering coffee cans with paper. I used foil wrapping paper for Christmas drumming with preschoolers and they have lasted for twenty years. Plasticized shelf paper would be even better. Cylindrical potato chip containers make smaller, manageable drums that can tuck under an arm.

Your main problem with drumming is control. When I pass out the drums, I ask that no one play their drum until we are all ready to begin. When I raise my hand the group drums. When I lower it, they stop. We practice this so that they are accustomed to following a leader. This also gives them a chance to beat their drums wildly and make a racket. Then we are ready to play and drum our story in a more controlled manner (hopefully).

Drumming stories can also be played out by drumming on one's legs. While using coffee-can drums is fun, they are cumbersome to carry and a nuisance to pass out and collect. Just drumming on table-tops, legs, books, or anything that makes a good sound works fine.

Here is a list of other tales with drumming possibilities, along with two of my own favorite drumming tales.

Tales to drum:

The Little Drummer Boy by Ezra Jack Keats, words and music by Katherine Davis, Henry Onorate, and Harry Simeone (New York: Aladdin Books, 1987). This story makes a sweet Christmas drumming activity for preschoolers. I instruct them to drum only when my hand is raised and stop immediately when it is lowered. I sing the story while showing the picture book. At each refrain 'rum pa pum pum,' I raise one hand and the children all drum. Then I lower my hand, they stop, and we proceed.

The Cat's Purr, written and illustrated by Ashley Bryan (New York: Atheneum, 1985). Rat plays sick while Cat works. But Rat gets up to play Cat's drum. Retold from a Montserrat tale that is included in the tale notes. Hear Ashley tell it on *Ashley Bryan: Poems & Folktales* (Belfast, Maine: Audio Bookshelf, 1994).

The Dancing Granny by Ashley Bryan (New York: Atheneum, 1980). See especially Ashley's audiotape *The Dancing Granny and Other African Stories* (New York: Caedmon, 1989). Anansi sings and drums to make Granny dance.

"A Drum" in *Tales Alive!* by Susan Milord (Charlotte, Vt.: Williamson, 1995), 37–45. She includes suggestions for turning a tale into a drumming story.

"Poule and Roach" from *Celebrate the World* by Margaret Read MacDonald (New York: H.W. Wilson, 1994), 32–42. Here Roach plays while his cockroach buddies party. Rabid drumming. We usually do this one as a leg-slapping dance. In a small group over which I have good control, I let the kids jump up and dance along with the song. Hear this on *Cockroach Party!* audiotape by Margaret Read MacDonald and Richard Scholz (Bellingham, Wash.: Live Music Recordings, 1999).

"Ttimba" in *Songs and Stories from Uganda* by W. Moses Serawadda (New York: Crowell, 1974). This is the story of a Lizard who steals Python's drum. Lizard sings and drums throughout in a refrain the kids can easily join. As this piece calls for really violent drumming, I usually ask the audience to do it with two fingers on their desk tops or by slapping their legs.

Drumming story collection:

Patakín: World Tales of Drums and Drummers by Nina Jaffe (New York: Henry Holt, 1994). Includes ten tales about drums with commentary on drumming. Not an easy source to adapt, but the dedicated drummer will find material here.

Fari Mbam

A Wolof Folktale from Gambia

There was a donkey king by the name of Fari Mbam.
All the donkeys lived together in the town of Jolof
and Fari Mbam was their King.

Now it happened that Fari grew tired of the company of donkeys.

He decided to visit the towns of the Wolof people
and live as a human for a while.

So he tucked in his ears,
tucked in his tail,
struck his hoof on the ground three times…
        REK REK REK…
and turned into a man.

Fari Mbam traveled through the town of Kaolack.
He traveled through the town of Ndofan,
He traveled through the town of Nyoro
He came to the town of Bati Hai
There a beautiful young girl smiled at Fari Mbam.
And Fari Mbam smiled back.

Fari Mbam married.
He stayed in Bati Hai.

Fari Mbam had one, two, three, four, *five* sons.
When the oldest son was fifteen,
Fari Mbam was still living in Bati Hai.

The Donkey people of Jolof were worried.
        "We need our *king*.
        Where has Fari Mbam gone?
        Why hasn't Fari Mbam returned?"

The Donkey people set out to find their lost king.
The first thing they all did was…
tuck in their ears…
tuck in their tails…
stamp their hooves on the ground three times…
            Rek Rek Rek…
and turn themselves into men.
Each man took a drum and they traveled
to the town of Kaolack.
When they reached the marketplace,
they set up their drums and began to sing.
            "Fari Mbam! *Dum-te-dum*!
            Fari Mbam! *Dum-te-dum*!
            Where's that DON-key?
            Fari Mbam? *Dum-te-dum*!"

They sang until a crowd gathered.
But then the donkey people forgot themselves.
They raised their noses in the air and began to bray!
            "Fari Mbam! *Nya-hunh! Nya-hunh*!
            Fari Mbam! *Nya-hunh! Nya-hunh*!
            King of the DON-keys!
            Fari Mbam! *Nya-hunh! Nya-hunh*!"

The crowd was excited.
What drumming!
What singing!
How can they *sing* like that?

One man spoke to them.
            "I think I have heard of this Fari Mbam
            There is a man in Bati Hai with that name.
            But I don't think he's going to like being called a *donkey*."

The donkey people stamped their feet and bowed.
            "Thank you. Thank you.
            Peace be *with* you."
They hurried down the road in the direction of Bati Hai.

Till they reached Ndofan.
There they stopped in the marketplace
and began to sing and drum.

"Fari Mbam! *Dum-te-dum*!
Fari Mbam! *Dum-te-dum*!
Where's that DON-key?
Fari Mbam! *Dum-te-dum*!"

Again they lost control.
"Fari Mbam! *Nya-hunh! Nya-hunh*!
Fari Mbam! *Nya-hunh! Nya-hunh*!
King of the DON-keys!
Fari Mbam! *Nya-hunh! Nya-hunh*!"

A man spoke up.
"I know this Fari Mbam of whom you speak.
He lives in the village of Bati Hai.
He is married to a beautiful woman.
But you shouldn't call him a donkey!"

The donkey people looked at one another.
"Our king is *married*?"
They thanked the villagers of Ndofan and hurried on.
"Thank you…thank you…
Peace be *with* you."

When they came to the village of Nyoro,
they began at once to drum and sing.
"Fari Mbam! *Dum-te-dum*!
Fari Mbam! *Dum-te-dum*!
Where's that DON-key?
Fari Mbam! *Dum-te-dum*!
But they couldn't contain themselves.
"Fari Mbam! *Nya-hunh! Nya-hunh*!
Fari Mbam! *Nya-hunh! Nya-hunh*!
King of the DON-keys!
Fari Mbam! *Nya-hunh! Nya-hunh*!"

In this village, several people spoke up.
"Yes…we know this Fari Mbam.
He lives just in the next village at Bati Hai.
He is married to a beautiful woman.
And he has five sons.
But he won't like being called a donkey!"

"What is this? Our king has *five sons*?"

The donkey people looked at one another.
"Thank you…thank you…
Peace be *with* you."

They hurried to Bati Hai.
They set up their drums in the marketplace.
Now they were so excited!
They forgot to even *try* to sing like humans.
"Fari Mbam! *Nya-hunh! Nya-hunh!*
Fari Mbam! *Nya-hunh! Nya-hunh!*
King of the DON-keys!
Fari Mbam! *Nya-hunh! Nya-hunh!*"

Inside his house, Fari Mbam heard this singing.
"My people have come!" he said to his wife.
I must go to them!"

"No. No," said his wife.
"You might not come back!
Then I will be so alone."

So Fari stayed inside his house.

The donkey people were drumming and calling.
"Fari Mbam! *Nya-hunh! Nya-hunh!*
Fari Mbam! *Nya-hunh! Nya-hunh!*
King of the DON-keys!
Fari Mbam! *Nya-hunh! Nya-hunh!*"

"Wife, I cannot help myself!" said Fari Mbam
"I am tingling all over!
I must go!"

And he ran from the house into the marketplace.
"Here I *come*!
Fari Mbam!"
Fari Mbam stomped his foot on the ground…
REK REK REK…
His foot became a hoof.
REK REK REK…
Out popped his ears!
REK REK REK…
Out popped his tail!

Rᴇᴋ Rᴇᴋ Rᴇᴋ…
He had turned to a DON-key.

Inside the house, Fari Mbam's sons became excited.
"Father's people have come!
We must go to them."

"No. No," said the mother.
"If you leave also, I will be so sad."

But the sons could hear those donkeys calling.
"Fari Mbam! *Nya-hunh! Nya-hunh!*
Fari Mbam! *Nya-hunh! Nya-hunh!*"

"Mother, we cannot help ourselves.
We are tingling all over."

They ran from the house into the marketplace.
"Fari Mbam!
Fari Mbam!"
Rᴇᴋ Rᴇᴋ Rᴇᴋ…
They stomped their feet on the ground.
Rᴇᴋ Rᴇᴋ Rᴇᴋ…
Their feet became hooves.
Rᴇᴋ Rᴇᴋ Rᴇᴋ…
out popped their ears.
Rᴇᴋ Rᴇᴋ Rᴇᴋ…
out popped their tails.
Rᴇᴋ Rᴇᴋ Rᴇᴋ…
They had turned into *DON-keys*!

"Fari Mbam! *Nya-hunh! Nya-hunh!*
Fari Mbam! *Nya-hunh! Nya-hunh!*
King of the DON-keys!
Fari Mbam!"

How the donkey people rejoiced.
They sang and danced all the way back home.
"Fari Mbam! *Nya-hunh! Nya-hunh!*
Fari Mbam! *Nya-hunh! Nya-hunh!*
King of the DON-keys!
Fari Mbam! *Nya-hunh! Nya-hunh!*"

The Wolof people tell us,
Be careful who you marry.
Don't ever wed a stranger.
He might turn out to be a DON-key.

Tips for telling:

It is fun to encourage your audience to bray and drum with you as you tell the story. On repeated tellings, they may want to jump up and dance as well. I pronounce "Mbam" "Mmm-Bäm" so that the "a" in "Fari" and "Mbam" are both like the "a" in "father." In "King of the DON-keys" "DON-key" sounds almost like a bray.

About the story:

This story may be found as "The Donkeys of Jolof" in *Folk Tales from the Gambia: Wolof Fictional Narratives* by Emil A. Magel (Three Continents Press, 1984), 154–57. It was recorded in Bati Hai, The Gambia by Lamin Jeng, age thirty-one. Magel tells us that Lamin Jeng is a noted griot, who in this case was performing at his father's home for seventeen adult men and women. The author explains that Fari-Mbam translates as "Donkey King" but with the added meaning that this king is a descendent of royalty on both his mother's and father's side. See Magel for more notes on this tale.

This story includes Motif *D332.11 Transformation: ass (donkey) to person; B641.4 Marriage to person in ass form* (Stith Thompson cites a Hausa variant of *B641.6 Marriage to person in horse form*); *B221 Animal kingdom-quadruped*; *B211.1.3.2 Speaking Mule* (Stith Thompson cites a Kordofan variant); and *D786.1 Discenchantment by song* (Stith Thompson cites a Swazi variant).

The Big Man Drum
A Dai Folktale from China

Yan worked for the rich farmer, Xiti.
Xiti treated Yan badly and made him work very hard.

One day, Yan was high in the mountains chopping wood.
After lunch he stretched out in the sun.
While Yan was lying there with his eyes closed,
a band of monkeys came leaping out of the forest.

They saw Yan and stopped.
      "What *is* it?"

      "It's a *man*."

      "It doesn't move. Maybe it's a statue."

Yan heard the monkeys chattering.
He lay very still to see what they would do.
The monkeys gathered around and began to poke at him.
One poked his fingers in Yan's ear.
Yan did not move.
      "It's a statue."
Another poked his fingers in Yan's mouth.
Yan did not move.
      "It's a statue."
Another monkey pulled up Yan's eyelids
and peered into his eye.
Yan did not move.
      "It's a statue."
A monkey poked his finger up Yan's nose!
Still Yan did not move.
      "It's a statue all right."

Then one of the monkeys hit Yan hard,
right in the middle of his stomach!
The blow forced air out of Yan's throat: "Unnh!"

"Oh!" The monkeys all jumped back.
"Now we know what it is!
It's a *drum*!
It's a Big Man Drum!"

The monkeys all clustered around
and began to beat on their Big Man Drum.

Every time they socked him in the stomach,
Yan grunted, "Unh!"
"Unh! Unh!
Unh-unh-unh!"
The monkeys were delighted with their new drum.
"Let's take our Big Man Drum home to our cave!"
They carefully picked Yan up.
Many monkeys helped so he would not be dropped.
One little monkey rode on top of Yan's stomach
to play the Big Man Drum!
They danced off home.
"We've got a Big Man Drum!
We've got a Big Man Drum!
Unh! Unh! Unh! Unh!
Unh! Unh! Unh!
We've got a Big Man Drum!"

Up the mountain they danced.
Now the monkeys had built a bridge of vines
over a deep river they had to cross.
When they came to the bridge of vines,
they held Yan very carefully
"Don't drop the Big Man Drum.
Don't drop the Big Man Drum.
Unh! Unh! Unh! Unh!
Unh! Unh! Unh!
Don't drop the Big Man Drum."

Yan held very still.
He did not want to be dropped into the rushing river.
Then on up the mountain charged the excited monkeys.

"We've got a Big Man Drum!
We've got a Big Man Drum!
Unh! Unh! Unh! Unh!
Unh! Unh! Unh!
We've got a Big Man Drum!"

They carried Yan into their cave
and set him up on their little stone altar.

"Let's make our Big Man Drum beautiful!
Go pick flowers!"

The monkeys ran out of the cave
and began to gather flowers.
They ran back to decorate their Big Man Drum.

They put flowers on his head,
flowers on his shoulders.
They filled his lap with flowers
and sprinkled flowers around his feet.

"Let's make our Big Man Drum *more* beautiful.
Let's cover him with *jewels*!"

The monkeys ran to their cubbies deep in the cave.
Soon they came running with armloads of jewels.

They hung Yan with necklaces and bracelets,
belts and anklets.
They crowned him with jewels,
filled his lap with jewels,
and lay jewels all around his feet.

"Now let's *play* our Big Man Drum!"
Unh! Unh! Unh! Unh!
Unh! Unh! Unh!"
The monkeys played and danced all around the cave.

When they were tired,
the monkeys went off to their cubbies to sleep.

As soon as they were sound asleep,
Yan climbed down from the altar.

He gathered up all of the jewels
and hurried back home.
He was *very* careful crossing the vine bridge.

The next day Yan sold some of the jewels.
Now he could buy a farm of his own.
He didn't have to work for rich Xiti any more.

But Xiti was jealous of Yan's new fortune.
He went to Yan's house one day and said:
>   "Birds are in pairs in the trees.
>   Carp are in pairs in the water.
>   Yan, why don't you marry my daughter?"

Yan knew that Xiti only wanted his money.
So he said, "This bird is happy alone."

Xiti pried and pried.
At last Yan explained where he found his riches.

Next day Xiti asked his wife to sew him a big bag,
big enough to carry treasure.
He climbed the mountain to the forest and lay down
in just the same spot where Yan had rested.

Here came the forest monkeys leaping along.
>   "Our Big Man Drum!
>   Our Big Man Drum came back!"
They began at once to pound their drum.
>   "*Unh! Unh! Unh!*
>   *Unh-unh-unh-unh-unh!*"

Xiti did not like being pounded.
His grunts sounded angry.

>   "Our drum doesn't sound the same anymore."

>   "Oh well. Let's take it home."

They picked Xiti up
and began to carry him back to their cave.
>   "Our Big Man Drum came back!
>   Our Big Man Drum came back!

Unh! Unh! Unh! Unh!
Unh! Unh! Unh!
Our Big Man Drum came back!"

Then they came to the vine bridge over the river.
"Careful! Don't drop our Big Man Drum!"

When Xiti heard that he became frightened.
"Be careful with our Big Man Drum!
Be careful with our Big Man Drum!
Unh! Unh! Unh! Unh!
Unh! Unh! Unh!
Be careful with our Big Man Drum!"

Xiti could feel himself swaying and swaying.
He had to see what was happening.
He opened one eye and looked down.
"AAAAHHHHH! Don't drop me!
Don't drop me!"

"It's *alive!*"
The terrified monkeys
tossed their Big Man Drum into the river.
Xiti the rich man was never seen again.

But Yan lived happily for the rest of his days.
One very contented bird in his own little nest.

As for the monkeys,
they never found a Big Man Drum again.
But sometimes they would gather in their cave,
pound their own little tummies,
and sing about him.
"Remember our Big Man Drum?
Remember our Big Man Drum?
Unh! Unh! Unh! Unh!
Unh! Unh! Unh!
We lost our Big Man Drum."

Tips for telling:

I lead the audience in pounding our tummies and grunting as the monkeys pound the man's tummy and make him grunt. We exhale in rhythm "Unh! Unh! Unh! Unh!...Unh! Unh! Unh!" This could also be performed while pounding on a drum, table top, book, the floor, etc.

About the story:

This is retold from "Monkeys Carrying a Big Drum" in *Folk Tales and Legends of the Dai People: the Thai Lue in Yunnan, China*, translated from Chinese text by Yung Yi, edited by John Hoskin and Geoffrey Walton (Bangkok: D.D. Books, 1992), 51–54. MacDonald Motif *J2415.23* Farmer disguised as scarecrow taken for Jizo statue by monkeys* cites two Japanese sources. In the Japanese version, the farmer is thought to be a Jizo statue and is taken to the cave and decorated.

Section Two

Talk-Back Tales

6 Stories with Improv Slots

SOME STORIES ARE STRUCTURED IN SUCH A WAY THAT the experienced teller can let the audience contribute data to the story, then incorporate this into the tale. I have seen tellers improvise entire stories based on audience suggestions. A clear sense of story structure plus a knack for improvised dialogue facilitates this. While I don't suggest this for the beginner, it *is* possible to let your audience in on story creation in smaller ways.

For example when telling the story "Forget-me-Not," a tale in which Adam names the flowers, I wander among the audience letting the children tell me which flower they are. Then I incorporate that flower next into the story.

To embark on stories with improv slots, you need a clear notion of the range of answers you are likely to receive from your audience. Just relax with the story and play with the audience. If someone throws you a totally off-the-wall suggestion either ignore it or just laugh and move on to something you can use. And don't feel bad because you can't think of some brilliant repartee. Your job is just to keep the story moving and facilitate playful activity with the audience. You don't have to be a stand-up comedian.

Here is a list of tales that lend themselves to this technique. If you find you enjoy this kind of story play, you will likely find others that work just as well. Below are two tales with improv-slot possibilities. "Buchettino" allows for simple contributions from the audience. Our small hero wants to eat a fruit that creates no garbage to toss away. The audience members make suggestions, which the teller incorporates into the story. "The Girl Who Wore Too Much" can include a much more extensive bout of playing with the audience. It is fun to move among the children letting them offer you more and more pieces of jewelry to wear. Encourage the children to tell you about the jewelry they are offering, then add each imaginary piece to your body as you get heavier and heavier with the burden of many jewels. This story was published as a picture book, *The Girl Who Wore Too Much: A Folktale from Thailand*, but in that format I was unable to show fully the story play possibilities of the tale, so I am repeating it here.

Stories with improv-slot possibilities:

"Forget-me-Not" in *Celebrate the World* by Margaret Read MacDonald (New York: H.W. Wilson, 1994), 83–88. Adam names the flowers.

"Mikku and the Trees" in *Earth Care: World Folktales to Talk About* by Margaret Read MacDonald (North Haven, Conn.: Linnet, 1999), 22–27. Trees object to being cut. Teller addresses audience members as trees. Asks each why it should not be cut.

"Mrs. Mondry and Her Little Dog" by Anne Pellowski in *Joining In* compiled by Teresa Miller (Cambridge, Mass.: Yellow Moon, 1988), 67–70. A tale to tease the audience. Pellowski encourages the audience to finish her phrases for her, then surprises them with something completely different from the phrase she has led them to produce.

"Turtle of Koka" in *The Storyteller's Start-Up Book* by Margaret Read MacDonald (Little Rock: August House, 1993), 111–16. The story has a simple structure and chant. Turtle claims nothing can cut his shell. Audience members suggest implements to try on him. He sings saucily back to each.

"Teeny-Weeny Bop" in *Look Back and See: Twenty Lively Tales for Gentle Tellers* by Margaret Read MacDonald (New York: H.W. Wilson, 1991), 147–56. This is actually a faux improv-slot tale. I pretend to be taking suggestions from the audience as I tell this. But in fact I know exactly which animals I want to use in the story. I encourage the audience members to keep shouting out pets the Teeny-Weeny Bop might buy. Then I select the one I wanted to use all along. If they are all shouting loudly I can pretend I heard it even if I didn't. If no one says the animal I want to use and they are quiet enough that I would be caught, I can always say, "Oh what if I bought a...!" and go on.

"A Penny and a Half," see page 114. Audience members can suggest which animals you buy in this story.

"The Singing Turtle" in *Look Back and See: Twenty Lively Tales for Gentle Tellers* by Margaret Read MacDonald (New York: H.W. Wilson, 1991), 137–45. Audience members suggest what songs the turtle can sing. The cat song? Dog song? He then sings in the voice of that animal.

"Little Snot Nose Boy" in *Celebrate the World* by Margaret Read MacDonald (New York: H.W. Wilson, 1994), 104–14. Woodcutter given wishes by snot-nose boy. Audience suggests things he can wish for.

"The War Between the Sandpipers and the Whales" in *Peace Tales: World Folktales to Talk About* by Margaret Read MacDonald (Hamden, Conn.: Linnet, 1992), 39–47. Sandpiper and whale fight. Each calls more of its kind to come aid in the battle. Audience suggests which birds and sea creatures are called. This can go on for a very long time as they think of more and more creatures to call.

The Girl Who Wore Too Much

*A Pu-Thai Folktale from Isaan
(Northeastern Thailand)*

Aree's parent gave that girl everything she wanted.
They showered that girl with gifts.

If she saw earrings in a jewelry shop,
her mother would say,
>"Oh Aree!
>Those earrings would look so attractive on your dainty ears.
>We must *buy* them for you!"

If she saw a bracelet in a jewelry shop,
her father would say,
>"Oh Aree!
>That bracelet would look so sweet on your little arm.
>We must *buy* it for you!"

If she saw a ring in a jewelry shop,
her parents would both say,
>"Oh Aree!
>That ring would look so fine on your slender finger.
>We must *buy* it for you!"

And whenever they saw an especially beautiful silk,
>"Oh *Aree*!
>That silk would look *so* lovely on you.
>We must *buy* it for you!"

Aree's room was stuffed with boxes of jewels.
She had chests full of silk.
But where could she *wear* all this finery?

Then she heard of a *dance*
in the village beyond the mountains.

"Now I can show off all of my fine clothes!
I'm going to be...
The most beautiful girl at the dance!

But which silk should I wear?
The red? It is *so* beautiful.
Or the pink?
But look at this *blue*!"

At this point pretend to show the silks to your audience and ask rhetorically, "Which should I wear? Don't you like this red? But what about this blue?" After going on like this for a while end with...

"I think I'll wear...
the *pink*!"
And she put on a pasin of bright pink silk.
"Just *look* at me!
I'm going to be...
the most beautiful girl at the dance!

But look at this green silk!
Oh...it is *so* beautiful.
Maybe I should wear *it*.
Nooo...I know!
I could wear them *both*!"

And she quickly put the green on top of the pink!

"Now I can show off *two* of my fine dresses.
I'm going to be...
The Most Beautiful Girl at the Dance!

Oh look at this fuschia! It is *so* bright.
What do you think?...*(holding pretend dress up)*
Why *not*? I'll wear it too!"

And she put the fuschia...
right on top of the other two dresses!
"Just *look* at me!
The Most Beautiful Girl at the Dance!"

Twirl around and show off all your dresses. Continue putting dress over dress in this fashion. Ask the audience each time whether you should wear it or not. Then put it on anyway. Twirl and brag. Move ever more slowly as you get bundled up in layers of clothing. You can brag about how no one else has expensive silk like this. At last you can hardly move at all.

> "Well it *is* a bit hard to move.
> But just *look* at me.
> The Most Beautiful Girl at the Dance!
>
> Now.
> Which bracelet shall I wear?
> The silver? The gold? The jade?"

Put on a couple of pretend bracelets and then ask the audience if they have any bracelets for you. This time actually interact with them. Walk around asking, "What kind of bracelet do you have?" The child will make something up. "A gold one." "Oh I like that! Thank you!" Pretend to load your arms with these bracelets.

> "Aren't I beautiful!
> But what about rings? I don't have any rings!"

Repeat the routine with the audience and fill your fingers with rings.

> "Well it *is* a bit hard to lift my arms now.
> But I'm *certain* to be
> The Most Beautiful Girl at the Dance!
>
> Now let's see. What else do I need?"

You can add necklaces, earrings, tiaras, if you like. Take it as far as the audience wants to go. Add one item at a time.

> "I think I am *ready*!
> How do I *look*? (*Twirl to show off.*)
> Don't you think I will be…
> The Most Beautiful Girl at the Dance!"

When her friends arrived
they could hardly believe their eyes.
Aree was covered with bracelets, necklaces,
earrings, dresses…
She looked *so* silly.

"Aren't I beautiful?
I'm certain to be…
The Most Beautiful Girl at the Dance!"

Her friends didn't know what to say.
They tried not to laugh.
They started off for the dance.
But the path led up a hill.
Poor Aree could not keep up.
In her heavy clothes she could hardly walk.

"Wait for me! Wait for me!
I can't get up the hill!" *(waddling)*

Her friends came back.
"Perhaps we could *push* you up the hill."

"Don't *push*. You'll wrinkle my dresses."

"Perhaps we could *pull* you up the hill."

"Don't *pull*. You'll soil my fine clothes!"

So her friends went on.
But soon Aree was calling again.
"Wait for me! Wait for me!
I can't get up the hill!"

Her friends went back once more.
"Aree, take off some of your jewelry!
Take off some of your clothes!
then you can climb the hill."

"Oh no. That's what you *want* me to do.
Then I won't be…
The Most Beautiful Girl at the Dance."
She refused to take off anything at all.

So her friends left her there.
They went on to the dance without her.

All day in the hot sun Aree trudged up the hill.
By nightfall she had just reached the top.

She collapsed there…stuck in her heavy clothes.
Too exhausted to take another step.

When her friends returned from the dance,
Aree was still too tired to move.
So they sent for her parents to carry her home.

By the time her parents arrived,
Aree was vain no more.
>"Mother, Father, I wore too much.
>I don't need all of these clothes."

>"Then take off some of your dresses.
>Take off those heavy jewels.
>We have taught you to want too much.
>You must learn to be happy with less."

So jewel by jewel, dress by dress
Aree gave away all of those things.

And the next time she went to a dance,
she was lovely in one simple dress.

Tips for telling:

As I pretend to put dresses on, one after the other, I keep twirling and saying that I am going to be the "most beautiful girl at the dance." When you begin putting on jewelry, the story can be drawn out for a very long time as you ask the audience to hand over pretend bracelets, rings, necklaces, etc. Sometimes it works to hand the jewelry and dresses back at the story's end when Aree gives everything away. If the audience is getting rousty, skip this step and just close the story. Try to find a copy of the picture book so you can share the pictures with your audience too. It could be nice to tell the story first and then show the pictures or read it again showing the illustrations. Great care was taken to make the illustrations as accurate as possible. The picture book is bilingual, with a fine Thai text.

For a follow-up activity, I photocopy the girl from the book's cover (enlarging it slightly), then cut her out to make a paper doll. I cut three skirts of varying lengths to go on the doll. Then I make photocopies of the girl and her skirts to give the children. They can color the skirts any colors they wish.

About the story:

For a picture book version of this story, see *The Girl Who Wore Too Much: A Folktale from Thailand*, Thai text by Supaporn Vathanaprida, illustrated by Yvonne LeBrun Davis (Little Rock: August House, 1998). The story was inspired by a tale in Kermit Krueger's *The Serpent Prince: Folktales from Northeastern Thailand* (New York: World, 1969) and was elaborated with the aid of Wajuppa Tossa, Supaporn Vathanaprida, and other Thai and Phu-Thai friends. The story's ending has been softened. The tale is said to be based on fact, and the girl actually expired on the hilltop. A small stone monument marks the spot and the hill bears her name. For more background information on this story, see "The Girl Who Wore Too Much: In Search of Authenticity in the Folktale Picture Book" in *Book Links* (September 1998, 46–49). This is Motif *W116 Vanity*.

Buchettino

A Folktale from Italy

Buchettino was such a good little boy.
Everything his Mama told him to do, he did.
If his Mama said, "Buchettino, go feed the dog,"
Buchettino went right away and fed the dog.
He never had to be told twice.

If his Mama said,
       "Buchettino, go and water the flowers,"
Buchettino went right away and watered the flowers.

One day Buchettino's Mama said,
       "Buchettino dear,
       would you go down and sweep the stairs for Mama?"
Buchettino didn't have to be told twice.
He went right down with his little broom.
He swept and he swept and he swept…
and while he was sweeping…
Buchettino found a *coin*!
       "What *luck*!
       I will go to the market
       and buy myself something good to eat!"

Buchettino put away his little broom
and went right down to the marketplace.
       "I want something *good* to eat.
       What shall I buy?
       I know. I will buy an *apple*!
       I *like* apples.
       No. I would have to throw away the *core*.
       I don't want to make garbage.

       "I'll buy a *banana*!
       I *like* bananas.

No. I would have to throw away the peeling.
I don't want to make garbage.

"I'll buy an *orange*!
Yes, I *like* oranges.
Oh no. I would have to throw away the peel
and the seeds too.
I don't want to make garbage.

"I *know*!
I will buy a *fig*!
Then I can eat the whole thing!"

Buchettino went to the fig merchant and bought a little bag of figs.
He took his bag of figs home and climbed a pear tree.
Then he began to eat the figs.
Just then…down the road came…*Old Man Ogre*!

"Why there is that fat, fat little Buchettino!
Wouldn't *he* make a tasty supper for me tonight?
Let's see if I can get him into my bag."
Old Man Ogre came up to the pear tree.
He began to call.
"Dear little Buchettino…
Hand me down a fig with your dear little hand."

But Buchettino was not so easily fooled.
"No…no…no…I won't hand you down a fig.
You might catch me and stuff me into your bag.
But I *will* share."
Buchettino threw a fig down.
He threw it so hard it rolled off down the hill,
and while Old Man Ogre was chasing after it,
Buchettino jumped down from the tree,
ran into the house, and closed the door.

His Mama said,
"Dear little Buchettino, how clever you *are*!"
And she put a candy in his mouth.

But Old Man Ogre said,
"That Buchettino tricked me today.
But he won't trick me *tomorrow*."

The next day, Buchettino's Mama called him and said,
     "Buchettino dear,
       would you go out and sweep the stairs?"
Buchettino didn't have to be told twice.
He took his little broom
and began to sweep the stairs.
He swept and he swept and he swept and…
guess what he found?
A *coin*!
     "What *luck*!
     I will go to market
     and buy something good to eat!"
Buchettino put away his broom and went to market.

     "What shall I buy today?
     Maybe a *plum*!
     I *like* plums.
     No. I would have to throw away the pit.
     I don't want to make garbage.

     "I could buy a *mango*!
     I *like* mangos.
     But I would have to throw away the big seed.
     I don't want to make garbage.

     "I *know*!
     I'll buy *raisins*!
     I can eat the whole thing!"

So Buchettino bought a bag full of raisins.
He went to sit in his pear tree and eat them.
It wasn't long before along came…
Old Man Ogre!

     "There is that fat, fat little Buchettino
     up in his tree again.

     Dear little Buchettino,
     hand me a raisin with your dear little hand."

     "Oh-*no*! I won't hand you down a raisin.
     You might grab me and put me in your bag!
     But I will share."

Buchettino threw down a raisin.
But it fell in the dirt.

"Buchettino, you wicked child.
The raisin fell into the dirt.
Hand me down a raisin with your dear little hand."

"Oh-*no*! I won't hand it down with my little hand.
You might grab me and put me into your bag.
But I will share."
And Buchettino threw down another raisin.
This raisin fell in the dirt too.

"Buchettino, you wicked little boy.
You are *wasting* food!
Now hand a raisin down to me in your *hand*!"

Little Buchettino didn't want to waste food.
So he handed a raisin down…
and Old Man Ogre *grabbed* Buchettino,
popped him into his bag
and carried him off home.
"Buchettino…Buchettino…
Yummy Nummy Buchettino…

"Wife *come out*!
See what I have brought for *supper*!"
He set the bag down by the door
and went to fetch his wife.
But as soon as the Ogre was gone,
Buchettino pulled out his little pocket knife,
cut a hole in the bag, and climbed out.

"Legs, it is no shame
to run away when there is danger,"
said Buchettino.
"Run little legs…*run*!"
And his little legs *ran* for home, raced inside,
and Buchettino closed the door.

"Buchettino, what a clever boy!" said his Mama.
And his Mama put a candy in his mouth.

But Old Man Ogre said,
          "That Buchettino tricked me today,
          but he won't trick me *tomorrow*!"

The next day, Buchettino's Mama said,
          "Buchettino dear,
          would you go out and sweep the stairs?"
Buchettino didn't have to be told twice.
He took his little broom and went to the stairs.
He swept and he swept and he swept and...
...guess what he found?
A *coin*!
          "What *luck*!
          I will go to the market
          and buy something good to eat!"
He put away his little broom
and went down to the market.

          "What shall I buy to eat today?
          Maybe a *peach*!
          I *like* a peach.
          No. I would have to throw away the pit.
          I don't want to make garbage.

          "I could buy a slice of *watermelon*!
          I *love* watermelon.
          I would have to spit out seeds
          and throw away the rind.
          I don't want to make garbage.

          "I *know*!
          I'll buy *blueberries*!
          I can eat the whole thing."

So Buchettino bought a bag of blueberries.
He took them home, but he said,
          "That pear tree is too dangerous.
          I will eat them *higher*."
Buchettino went up on the *roof* of his house.
He climbed up the ladder at the back,
then he scooted himself out to the front of the roof,
so he could look down at the people on the road.

It wasn't long before
along came *Old Man Ogre*!

"Dear little Buchettino,
hand me down a blueberry with your little hand."

"Oh-*no*! I won't hand you down a blueberry.
You might grab me and pop me into your bag again."

"Buchettino…" said Old Man Ogre.
"Tell me,
how did you get up on that roof so high?"

"Oh I climbed up the…"
Buchettino almost gave himself away.
But he was too clever for that.

"It was easy," said Buchettino.
"I piled glasses upon glasses
plates upon plates
pots upon pots
and pans upon pans.
Then I climbed up."

"Ohhhh," said Old Man Ogre. "I see."

Old Man Ogre went to the market.
He bought glasses.
He bought plates.
He bought pots.
He bought pans.

Old Man Ogre came back.
He put glasses on glasses.
He put plates on plates.
He put pots on pots.
He put pans on pans.

Old Man Ogre began to climb up that pile.
And when he reached the top…
why that pile began to tipple and topple and
Old Man Ogre *fell* to the ground and cracked his head!

"That *Buchettino*!
He tricked me yesterday.
He tricked me the day before.
And he tricked me *today*.
I'll bet he would like to trick me *tomorrow too*!
But he won't get the chance.
Because I'll not come back *here*!"
And Old Man Ogre stumbled off, holding his head.

Buchettino climbed down from the roof.
He got out his little broom.
And he swept and he swept and he swept…
Buchettino swept up the broken glass
and put it in the garbage can.
He picked up the broken plates
and put them in the garbage can.
He gathered up the pots and pans
and carried them up the stairs.
          "Look Mama! Look what Old Man Ogre left us!"

          "Why, Buchettino,
          what a clever little boy you are!" said his Mama.
And his Mama put a candy in his mouth.
And a candy in each hand.
And she gave him such a *hug*!

Tips for telling:

You can, if you like, invite the children to help you sweep with Buchettino. Let Buchettino ask the children for help in thinking of a fruit that will not make garbage. Though some parents might object, it is nice to give each child a small piece of hard candy as a treat after telling this story.

About the story:

Versions of this story appear as "Buchettino" in *Italian Popular Tales* by Thomas Frederick Crane (Boston: Houghton Mifflin, 1885), 265–67, and as "Gianni and the Ogre" in *Gianni and the Ogre* by Ruth Manning-Sanders (New York: Dutton, 1970), 7–12. MacDonald's *Storyteller's Sourcebook* cites this as *G501F Stupid Ogre. Gianni and the Ogre. Gianni fills ogre's bag with stones and flees (K526). Ogre eats before discovering trick. Gianni says he climbed stack of plates to reach church steeple. Ogre tries and falls. Glasses-repeat. Bottles-ogre reaches tower and Gianni kicks bottles over. Ogre killed.* It contains Motif *K526 Captive's bag filled with animals or objects while captive escapes.* This is a variant of Type *327 C The Devil (Witch) Carries the Hero Home in a Sack.*

7 Riddle Stories

WHEN TELLING RIDDLE STORIES, IT OFTEN WORKS WELL to present the puzzle and then pause to let audience members venture guesses. This calls for you, the teller, to be alert, thinking on your feet in response to the various suggestions. And always be prepared for the eventuality that someone actually *guesses* the right answer. The trick to keeping such riddle tales engaging is to move the "guess the answer" sequence along rapidly. Call on listeners who look as if they actually have an answer on the tip of their tongue. Respond to them briskly but cheerily, "Sorry, that's not it," and move on to the next. And have your final comments well rehearsed as you reveal the right answer and conclude the story. You actually need two rehearsed endings for this…one if they do not guess the correct answer (as you hope will happen) and another in the rare case that they *do* guess the ending… which will sort of steal your thunder and require a different flash at the end.

I include two riddle tales here for you to begin with. George Shannon has written several collections of riddle stories that will serve as source for many more. At Mahasarakham University in Thailand, Dr. Wajuppa Tossa is using riddle tales to end each week's lunchtime storytelling program. The audience can talk about it among themselves until the next week when they hear the solution!

Riddling stories:

"Katchi, Katchi Blue Jay" in *Look Back and See* by Margaret Read MacDonald (New York: H.W. Wilson, 1991), 81. Puzzle story. How could Blue Jay have passed the snapping door?

"Riddle Story: In Summer I Die" by Doug Lipman in *Joining In* compiled by Teresa Miller (Cambridge, Mass.: Yellow Moon, 1988).

"Silly Riddle" in *Juba This and Juba That* by Virginia Tashjian (Boston: Little, Brown, 1995), 79. This story teases the audience with a silly ending sure to cause a groan.

Collections of Riddle Stories

The Cow of No Color: Riddle Stories and Justice Tales from Around the World by Nina Jaffe and Steve Zeitlin, illus. by Whitney Sherman (New York: Henry Holt, 1998).

More Stories to Solve: Fifteen Folktales from Around the World by George Shannon, illus. by Peter Sis (New York: Greenwillow, 1990).

Still More Stories to Solve: Fifteen Folktales from Around the World by Geroge Shannon, illus. by Peter Sis (New York: Greenwilow, 1994).

Stories to Solve: Fifteen Folktales from Around the World by George Shannon, illus. by Peter Sis (New York: Greenwillow, 1985).

True Lies: 18 Tales for You to Judge by George Shannon, illus. by John O'Brien (New York: Greenwillow, 1997).

The Rich Man Seeks
a Daughter-in-Law
A Folktale from Isaan (Northeastern Thailand)

There once was a rich man
whose son was of age to be married.
This man wanted his son to marry a good wife.
He did not care if she was rich.
He did not care if she was beautiful.
But he did care that she should be kind,
and good,
and wise.

So the rich man gave his son a question to ask of all the girls he met.

Here is the question:

> "If you had a big fish,
> how could you feed your family
> as long as possible?"

So the young man went out.
He asked every young woman he met this question.

> "If you had a big fish,
> how could you feed your family
> as long as possible?"

At this point let your audience make guesses. Let many people make suggestions. Reply to each: "I am sorry. That is not the right answer. You cannot marry the rich man's son."

At last the young man met a girl who looked interesting.
She was not incredibly beautiful.
She did not look rich.
But she did look kind and good.

So he asked her the question.

> "If you had a big fish,
> how could you feed your family
> as long as possible?"

This girl thought.
She said, "That is easy.
> First I would cook the fish with many vegetables.
> That way there would be a great deal of food.
> Then I would give some of the food to my relatives.
> I would give some of the food to my neighbors.
> I would give some of the food to my friends.
> Then when *they* had a big fish,
> they would bring some to share with me.
> That way this one big fish
> would feed my family for a long, long time."

This was the right answer.
So the young woman married the rich man's son.

And they lived happily ever after.

Tips for telling:

Take as long as you like in telling this story. Move among the audience, letting various persons guess at the riddle. While Thai audiences guess the answer quickly, it seldom occurs to Western audiences that sharing might be an answer. I like to tease the girls…"Sorry, you don't get to marry the rich man's son." I call on boys too for an answer, not just girls. They all like to have a chance at guessing.

About the story:

This tale was collected from Nai Tong Bai Pen Tong, age fifty-nine. He was a teacher at Nong Lek. He used to be a monk and passed the certification and was the abbot for sixteen years. He can speak and write Thai, Lao, and Khmer. He can tell every kind of story, including moral stories, Nithan Khati (teaching stories), Nithan Talok (humorous), Nithan Thamma (stories of the Dhamma) and others. The story was translated for me by Uraiwan Prabipu. My telling is shaped by hearing Uraiwan and Supawan Kaikaew tell this story many times. This is Motif *H388 Bride test: wisdom (cleverness)*, and *H552 Man marries girl who guesses his riddles*.

The Hare Who Married a Princess

A Fon Folktale from Benin

Retold from *Why Goats Smell Bad and Other Stories from Benin* by Raouf Mama.

My story takes flight over mountains and lakes...
over rivers and seas...
My story takes flight over forests...
...and alights on...
a princess!

There once was a princess so beautiful,
everyone wanted to marry her.
But her father, the king, wanted to keep her at home.

So the king devised a test.
Anyone who wanted to ask for the hand of the princess
must first drink from a pot of boiling water.

When the day of the test arrived, many suitors lined up.
First came a handsome prince from a neighboring country.

> "See me! I am brave and oh so gorgeous.
> Just watch me drink and win the beautiful princess."

He folded a cloth to lift the boiling clay pot.
He lifted the steaming pot to his lips...
but the steam raced up and burnt his nose!

> "Ahh!
> No! I cannot do this!"

And the handsome prince left in disgrace.

Another young man stepped forward.
He too lifted the steaming pot.

"Ahh!" His lips were burnt.
"Too hot! Too hot!"

He also left in disgrace.

And so it went with suitor after suitor.
At last every young man had tried.
And all had given up when the hot blast of steam hit their face.

So now the animals spoke up.

"Could we try too?
Perhaps one of *us* could marry the princess."

"Go ahead," said the king.
"Animals, birds, anyone brave is welcome to try."

Lion stepped up first.
With his thickly padded paws
he *was* able to lift the hot clay pot.
But when the steam went up his nose
he dropped it.

"Oh…I just changed my mind.
I don't want to get married today."

Lion left,
trying not to show his embarrassment.

Rhino, Giraffe, Monkey…all tried…
and all failed.

At last a small animal hopped to the king's throne.
"Sire, I would like to marry the princess."

The king looked down.
There was a tiny rabbit wriggling its nose.

"May I have a turn?
Let me try!"

"All right, little rabbit.
Go ahead and try."

Rabbit walked to the boiling pot.
He made a pad of cloth
so he could lift the pot without burning his hands.
He raised the pot high to the king...
and began to...*talk.*

> "Sire...I, Rabbit,
> am about to drink the hot hot water.
> I, Rabbit...am about to drink and die.
> I, Rabbit...am about to suffer excruciating death from
>   boiling water.
> Why...you ask...do I do this thing?
> Because I, Rabbit, love your daughter.
>
> "How *much* do I love her...you might ask?
> I love your daughter so much...
> that I am willing to drink this boiling water...
> to show my love for her.
>
> "Why would I drink such hot water and suffer sure
>   death
> to show my love for your daughter, you might ask?
>
> "Because this girl is so beautiful.
> Shall I name her beauty?
> She is beautiful in the hair...
> She is beautiful in the eye...
> She is beautiful in the nose...
> She is beautiful..."

Rabbit named all the girl's beautiful attributes.

> "*Now*,
> I...Rabbit...
> am about to drink this water.
> I...Rabbit...am about to die.
> *King*...I ask you...
> tell all of your children...
> of my brave deed.
> Tell your children's children...
> of my brave deed...
> Tell your children's children's children...
> of my brave deed...

Will you do this?…Good.

"Queen…I, Rabbit…
am about to drink this water.
I…Rabbit…am about to die.
I ask you…
Tell all of your children…of my brave deed.
Tell your children's children…
of my brave deed.
Tell you children's children's children…
of my brave deed.
Will you do this? You will. Good.

"Nobleman…I…Rabbit…
am about to drink this water.
I…Rabbit…am about to die.
I ask you, too…
tell all of your children…of my brave deed.
Tell you children's children…
of my brave deed.
Tell your children's children's children…
of my brave deed.
Will *you* do this? Good.

"Noblewoman…I…Rabbit…
am about to drink this water…"

Rabbit went slowly from person to person…
asking each to remember his bravery,
telling each of the beauty of the princess.
From time to time,
he cautiously dipped his finger into the pot.
At last Rabbit stopped and turned to the king.

"Now I, Rabbit,
drink from this boiling water
to *prove* my love for the *princess*!"

And quickly he downed the entire pot of water.

A *cheer* went up from the crowd!
He had done it! Rabbit had won the princess!

So Rabbit married the girl.

And to this day no one has dared to wonder...
just *how* he managed to drink boiling water.
But perhaps *you* know?

Tips for telling:

This is a "teasing-the-audience" story. Once Rabbit begins his
speechifying, I walk about through the audience...holding out his pot
of boiling water and asking them each in turn "...will *you* tell your
children? And your children's children..." I pause...lift the pot to my
lips as if to drink...then lower it and begin again. Usually individuals
will begin to call out "*Drink* it!" as they see what I am doing. Most
understand Rabbit's ploy long before the end.

This is an improv story of a different nature from those in Chapter
Six since you do not allow the audience to interject suggestions here.
You could, of course, memorize exactly what you wanted to say. But it
is more fun to just keep rattling away about the girl's beauty and the
audience's descendants. This is, in fact, the technique used by traditional bards that enabled them to tell for hours. They utilized such
"runs" or set strings of prose that they could return to again and
again. The format for the girl's beauties and the audience's descendants is set. Using this, you can just wander around the audience,
expanding the story as long as you wish.

About the story:

This story is retold from *Why Goats Smell Bad and Other Stories from
Benin*, translated and retold by Raouf Mama, illustrated by Imna
Arroyo (North Haven, Conn.: Linnet, 1998), 95–99. My retelling is published with the permission of Raouf Mama. I suggest that you consult
his text also before beginning to tell the tale. The story is from Raouf's
own Fon tradition. This is Motif *H221.4 Ordeal by boiling water.*

Section Three

Dramatic Play

8 Actors-from-the-Audience

SOME TELLERS HAVE DEVELOPED A TECHNIQUE IN WHICH audience members are invited onstage to take the parts of various characters as the teller narrates the story. This technique has advantages and disadvantages. The audience members onstage prove amusing to the audience and are immediate attention-catching devices. If the teller is skillful at improvisation much fun can be had with these folks as they put their own unique and often humorous interpretations into the story's characters. Such a tale can make a useful break in a long story program. The audience relaxes from the intensity of listening and just watches to see what the various audience members will do next. The story itself sometimes sacrifices, but the moment *is* playful.

Syd Lieberman has developed a successful use of this technique around the tale of the man who feels his home is too noisy. The Rabbi suggests that he get a dog, a cat, etc. In the end his house is *very* noisy. The Rabbi suggests that he take them all back. Now, what *peace*. Syd brings many audience members onstage to play the parts of barking dogs, meowing cats, and such. An easy-to-tell version of that tale is included in this chapter. I recommend that you also listen to Syd's "The Noisy House" on *Joseph the Tailor and Other Jewish Tales* (Little Rock: August House, 1999).

An artist who has taken this form to exceptional lengths is Andreanna Belcher. She can fill an entire hour with one *märchen,* bringing audience members onstage and encouraging them to speak their parts as well as act. Nearly half of her joke lines may come from these improv actors and her responses to them. While many tellers should be successful imitating Syd's simple re-enactment, I do not suggest that tellers attempt to imitate Andreanna's work. She works not with a formulaic tale but with lengthy folktales of the *märchen* fairy-tale variety. Her participants wander through the tale guided skillfully by Andreanna's artistry. This technique could easily turn to bumbling boredom in the hands of a less imaginative artist. But do see her work if you can. It is amazing and may inspire you to try bits of improv in smaller, more manageable ways.

Before you decide to subject your story to this treatment, consider the tale carefully.

- Does the tale have clear-cut characters with which audience actors can readily identify?

- Is the structure of the story obvious enough for your actors to sense where the story is going and what is required of them?

- Can you work around an "actor" who turns out to be unable to move and unwilling to speak?

- Will the heart of the story be distorted by the invasion of this irrelevant "acting out"?

- Would this story be more effective in a simple telling?

Warning: If you tell one story in this format, an audience of children will demand to take part in *all* of the stories you subsequently tell. Do not let your sense of each story's essence be swept away by this eagerness of your audience to turn *everything* into an "act-it-out" tale.

Uses: This technique *is* an attention-getting device. Once you master it and learn how to get audience members on and off stage quickly and keep the story flowing, you may find you enjoy it. If you can identify a couple of cooperative "actors," bringing actors on stage can sometimes engage a too-cool teen audience. This technique is *very* useful for the street performer. Stuck on a street-fair stage with no audience and minimal sound system, I found that bringing up a few children quickly drew a crowd of star hopefuls. A cheap trick maybe, but it worked.

Experiment with this in small informal groups. Do not attempt it onstage until you have developed a familiarity with the ramifications of this technique and the sudden pitfalls that can arise from a recalcitrant audience or a too-quirky actor.

Though I enjoy incorporating audience members into my stories at times, I often wonder if the story wouldn't have been more effective told without this distraction. And I definitely do not recommend this technique for every story, since it detracts from the flow of the story itself. Let me explain. I frequently use this technique when telling "Look Back and See," a Tanzanian folktale, which is in my book *Look Back and See: Twenty Lively Tales for Gentle Tellers* (New York: H. W. Wilson, 1991), 11–23. In this story a man, a woman, and a dog travel over the mountain to seek the dawn. After the man returns empty-handed the chief asks, "Can anyone in the village go? Who can bring back the dawn?" I often address this to the audience, select an audience member, and bring them up to go look for the dawn. I drape a necklace of cowrie shells around them (the chief sends shells to buy the dawn) and push them across the stage as the audience chants

"Eh eh eh eh She climbed the mountain." As the pattern of dialogue between the messenger and the chief who owns the dawn has been set up already in the first part of the story, I sometimes push the microphone at the "actor" and let them speak their own lines as they request some dawn. If I hit on a lively actor to perform the part of the little dog who finally brings back the dawn, the story moves well in this format. The technique works to rivet the attention of junior and senior high listeners, and I often use it in those venues. However, this is a fine and strong story with a dramatic flow that is beautiful in a simple telling. I always feel that the interruption of the story through this improvisation, though fun for the audience, does detract from their sense of the story and the deeper emotional impact of a simple telling. Will I keep utilizing this technique for this story? Probably. It's use makes a nice counterpoint in my fifty-minute program, gives them a relaxation from more intense story listening and allows me to take the audience deep into a quieter moment of introspection later with my telling of "Bear Child." Will I *always* incorporate such activity into this story? No. When telling to adults, when telling to younger children, or when telling one story only in a shorter venue, I let the story have the floor.

There are two stories in my repertoire that I never tell *without* incorporating audience-actors. They are "Ko Kongole" and "A Penny and a Half." See notes and sources for those below.

Stories for actors-from-the-audience:

"Fari MBam" (see p. 69). It can be fun to bring a small group of drumming donkeys onstage to join you in the search for Fari MBam.

"Ko Kongole" from *The Storyteller's Start-Up Book* by Margaret Read MacDonald (Little Rock.: August House, 1993), 179–84. This is a great participation piece with clapping and chanting for the entire audience and acting slots for as many as you want. The father brings suitors one by one for his daughter to admire. Each animal dances before her while the audience chants and claps. She rejects all. Finally Rooster is chosen. I play the part of the father and relate the story. I rehearse the audience in the chant before we begin and watch closely to see which of the women/girls is clapping on the beat. I select her as the princess. Anyone can play the other animal suitors, but I save one frisky looking young man to call on for the rooster at the tale's end. He gets to marry the princess and has opportunity for quite a bit of funny business should he so desire.

"Kudu Break!" in *The Storyteller's Start-Up Book* by Margaret Read MacDonald (Little Rock: August House, 1993). Wife #1 forces wife #3 to cook the turtle. Then wife #1 eats the turtle stew. Husband sets a test to find the culprit. Each wife must cross the river walking a rope of kudu skin. At this point in the story, I bring up two participants to hold the pretend rope and three wives to attempt crossing it. The rest of the audience make the sounds of the waves and the snapping turtles.

Mabela the Clever by Margaret Read MacDonald (Morton, Ill: Albert Whitman, 2000). Cat teaches mice to sing, then picks off those in the rear of marching line. I lead a few mice from the audience in this march while a "cat" accomplice snatches them up.

"The Magic Wings" by Diane Wolkstein in *Joining In* compiled by Teresa Miller (Cambridge, Mass.: Yellow Moon, 1988), 111–17. A Chinese tale of folks trying to grow wings to fly. Diane chooses a very light child as the little girl who succeeds. Thus she can actually fly her around the stage at the tale's end. In *Joining In* Wolkstein gives useful notes on how she "rehearses" her actors for the story. See also Diane's picture book, *The Magic Wings* (New York: Dutton, 1983).

"A Penny and a Half" in *Look Back and See: Twenty Lively Tales for Gentle Tellers* by Margaret Read MacDonald (New York: H.W. Wilson, 1991), 157–61. The audience joins in a chant, "I once found a penny and half. With my penny and half I bought a…" Audience members come up to act the parts of the animals we buy. Each animal gets to pick a baby animal to accompany it. Soon the front of the room is filled with mooing, barking, bellowing animals. In the last refrain we buy a guitar, and all of the animals dance. My students in Thailand loved this story and always ended it with a parade of animals as we danced around the room. My host there, Dr. Wajuppa Tossa, translated the tale into Lao, replaced the chant of the Chilean tale with a Lao folksong, and changed the guitar to a khaen, a local bamboo reed instrument. The result was more charming than ever! However, if you prefer to go nearer to the tale's roots, the Spanish version accompanies the story in *Look Back and See*.

"Rabbit at the Water Hole" adapted by Linda Goss in *Joining In* compiled by Teresa Miller (Cambridge, Mass.: Yellow Moon, 1988), 9–17. Lots of lively audience participation *and* audience-actors, as rabbit has many animals guarding the water hole.

"The Snooks Family" in *Juba This and Juba That* by Virginia Tashjian (Boston: Little, Brown, 1969), 39–41. Each family member tries to blow out the candle but all blow in a different direction. With its simple construction and facial contortions, this is an easy tale to adapt for the actors-from-the-audience technique.

"The Squeaky Door" in *A Parent's Guide to Storytelling* by Margaret Read MacDonald (HarperCollins, 1995), 35–41. I tell this as simple audience participation with lots of chiming in on the little boy's "No, not *me!*" but tandem tellers Jen and Nat Whitman have great fun bringing kids onstage to act the roles of barking, meowing, grunting animals in the bed.

The Little Old Woman
Who Hated Housework
Elaborated from Scottish Folk Tradition

There once was a little old woman who hated housework.
Every day she had to make her bed, do the dishes,
and sweep the floor.
Then she would sit down and work on her knitting.

One day when she was doing her dishes
she began to grumble.
> "Work! Work! Work!
> How I hate it! Hate it! Hate it!"

No sooner had these words left her mouth
than there came a knocking at the door.

> RAP RAP RAP!
> RAP RAP RAP!

A voice called out:
> "Your luck has come!
> Open the door!
> Let me in
> and you'll work no more!"

The little old woman opened the door…
and in rushed a little fairy lady.
She knocked the old woman aside,
bustled over to the sink,
and began to clatter and bang away at the dishes.

> *Klankety-klankety-klankety-klankety…*

> "Well, if she is going to do the dishes for me,
> I will sweep the floor."

The little old woman picked up her broom to sweep.
But soon she was grumbling again.
>"Work! Work! Work!
>How I hate it! Hate it! Hate it!"

And right away she heard:
>RAP RAP RAP!
>RAP RAP RAP!

>"Your luck has come!
>Open the door!
>Let me in
>and you'll work no more!"

She opened the door and
in came another little fairy lady.
The fairy lady pushed the old woman aside,
snatched up the broom,
and began to sweep dust all over the house!

>*Swishety-swishety-swishety-swishety…*

>"Well then, I guess I will make the bed."

The little old woman began to shake her bed covers.
But soon she was grumbling again.
>"Work! Work! Work!
>How I hate it! Hate it! Hate it!"

>RAP RAP RAP!
>RAP RAP RAP!

>"Your luck has come!
>Open the door!
>Let me in
>and you'll work no more!"

And when she opened the door,
a third little fairy lady knocked her aside,
bustled over to the bed
and began to shake the bedclothes.

>*Flumpety-flumpety-flumpety-flumpety…*

"Well that's nice.
Then I can sit down and knit."

But she hadn't been knitting long
before she began to grumble even about that.
"Work! Work! Work!
How I hate it! Hate it! Hate it!"

RAP RAP RAP!
RAP RAP RAP!

"Your luck has come!
Open the door!
Let me in
and you'll work no more!"

And another little fairy lady rushed in,
grabbed up the knitting,
and began to knit furiously.

Clickety-clickety-clickety-clickety...
Clickety-clickety-clickety-clickety...

Now the little old woman had no place to move.
She sat at the kitchen table.
The fairies swarmed around her.

Klankety-klankety-klankety-klankety...
swishety-swishety-swishety-swishety...
flumpety-flumpety-flumpety-flumpety...
clickety-clickety-clickety-clickety...

There was not a moment's peace in that house.
The little old woman sat there.
She sat there.
She was bored.
And she was annoyed.

"I'll help with the dishes and get them out of here,"
she thought.
But as soon as she reached for a plate,
the four fairies jumped on her
and pushed her back into the chair.

"Sit down! Sit down!
You'll work no more!"

She sat there for a while.
She was *very* bored.
She was *very* annoyed.
"I will just help with this sweeping."
But the moment she reached for a broom,
the four fairies leaped on her.
"Sit down! Sit down!
You'll work no more!"
The old lady was *increasingly* annoyed.
She was *excessively* bored.
"I will just help finish making that bed."

"Sit down! Sit down!
You'll work no more!"

"Well, at least I can do my knitting."

"Sit down! Sit down!
You'll work no more!"

They pushed her back into her chair.

*Klankety-klankety-klankety-klankety…
swishety-swishety-swishety-swishety…
flumpety-flumpety-flumpety-flumpety…
clickety-clickety-clickety-clickety…*

And then suddenly
the house was quiet.
The dishes were done.
The floor was swept.
The bed was made.
The knitting was finished.

The old woman breathed a sigh of relief.

And then…

"Change places! Change places!"

The fairies clapped their hands,
jumped up,
and all changed places!

The fairy who had been knitting
grabbed the broom,
and began to sweep the dust back over the floor.

The fairy who had been sweeping
pulled out the plates,
dumped them in the sink,
and began to dirty them up.

The fairy who had been doing dishes
ran to the bed and began to throw out the covers.

And the fairy who had been making the bed
yanked out the knitting needles,
and began to unravel the knitting.

As soon as everything was completely undone,
they cried:
             "Change places! Change places!"
And each fairy raced back and began doing the work all over again.

             Klankety-klankety-klankety-klankety...
             Swishety-swishety-swishety-swishety...
             Flumpety-flumpety-flumpety-flumpety...
             Clickety-clickety-clickety-clickety...

The old woman realized that they would *never* leave.

She would be surrounded by clicking and clacking
and swishing and flumpetying for the rest of her life!

She ran from her house.
She rushed to the town
and found the wise woman.

             "My house is overrun with fairies!"

             "Your house is overrun with fairies?
             Did you invite them in?"

"Well yes…"

"You hadn't been complaining, had you?"

"Well sort of…"

"Oh no! They've come to *help*.
You'll never be rid of them.
Well, here is what you must do.
Stand outside your door and shout,
'The hill is on fire!'
The fairy women will think their fairy mound is burning.
They will rush home to save their children.
As soon as they are gone,
you must go inside and bolt the door.
Then do just as I tell you.
Turn the broom upside down.
Put the dishes back in the sink all upside down.
Pull the bedcovers all apart and tangle them up.
Take out the needles and rip up the knitting.
And do it quickly.
For they will be back in a flash."

So the little old woman did just as she was told.

She stood outside the door and called, "The hill is on fire!"

"Our children! Our children!"
The fairy women *rushed* off to their fairy mound.

The little old woman ran inside and bolted the door.
She turned the broom upside down.
She put the dishes all back in the sink upside down.
She pulled the bedcovers apart and tangled them.
She took out the needles and ripped up the knitting.

And she had no sooner finished than

RAP RAP RAP!
RAP RAP RAP!
"Your luck is back!
Open the door!
Let us in
and you'll work no more!"

That old woman sat *so* still.
  Rap Rap Rap!
  Rap Rap Rap!
  "Your luck is back!
  Open the door!
  Let us in
  and you'll work no more!"

The little old woman did not move.

The fairies began to stir around and fuss.
  "Broom! Broom!
  Come open the door!"

But the broom called back:
  "I'm upside down!
  I cannot move!"

  "Dishes! Come let us in!"

  "We're upside down in the sink.
  We cannot come."

  "Bedcovers! Get up and come open the door!"

  "We're all tangled up.
  We cannot move."

  "Knitting! Get over here and open this door!"

  "Our needles are lost and our stitches are ripped!
  We cannot come."

Those fairies began to grumble and growl.
  "Then your luck is *gone*!
  We'll work no *more*!"
And they stomped away back to their fairy mound.

The little old woman got up.
She washed her dishes.
She swept her floor.
She made her bed.
Then she sat down and put her knitting back together again.

At long last she could rock and knit.

But soon she began to mumble.
"Work! Work! Work!...
...How I love it! Love it! Love it!"

Tips for telling:

The audience will soon join in on "RAP! RAP! RAP!" and the chant.
If you want to involve the audience even more, bring up an audience
member to act the role of each of the fairies. I incorporate these actors
at the point when all four are at work. I ask one to make the bed
"flumpety-flumpety," another to sweep the floor *"swishety-swishety,"*
another to do the dishes *"clackety-clackety,"* and the fourth to knit
"clickety-clickety." The audience members can join in on whichever
sound they like. I then act the part of the Little Old Woman. I try to get
the bed-maker to let me help. But I whisper to her to push me back
into my chair and instruct them all to shout at me, "Sit down! Sit
down! You'll work no *more!*" I repeat this with all four. The "Change
places!" takes a minute while I shuffle them all about, but the audience seems to like that. They rush off to check on the fire, then rush
back. Then they stomp off angrily, and I send them back to their
places in the audience while I finish the story in peace and quiet. The
story, of course, is perfectly delightful as a straight telling without all
this nonsense. But it *is* fun to play with it.

About the story:

MacDonald's *Storyteller's Sourcebook* cites this tale as *F381.8
Spinning fairies lured away from house by fire alarm.* She gives two
Scottish variants. The tale appears as "The Good Housewife and Her
Night Labors" in *Scottish Folk-Tales and Legends* by Barbara Ker Wilson
(Oxford: Oxford University Press, 1954), 115–20. Identical text
appears in *Favorite Fairy Tales Told in Scotland* by Virginia Haviland
(Boston: Little, Brown, 1963), 59–70. Wilson's old lady calls "Burg Hill
is on fire," and the fairies (both male and female) race off, calling the
names of the objects each fears might be burning up ("My big meal
chest!" "My butter kegs and cheese!"). A half-baked barley cake jumps
off the fire and runs to open to door, but she pinches it in two with
her fingers, and, since it is only half-baked, it collapses. She has turned
the spinning wheel, carding combs, distaff, loom, and fulling water
upside down already. She throws the fulling water on her sleeping husband, and he wakes and chases the fairies off. Leila Berg retells this
story as "Higgeldy-Piggledy and Topsy-Turvy" in *Folktales for Reading
and Telling* (New York: World, 1966), 88-95. She cites it as a Scottish
folktale and includes the chant "Ask me in, Ask me inner, I'll help you
if you give me dinner." Little old ladies (not described as fairies) come

in and eat her out of house and home. Her husband chases them off.

Related motifs are *F385.1 Fairy spell averted by turning coat* and *G272.9 Reversing the poker protects from witch*. The tale is clearly a variant of *F381.8.1* The Horned Women*. This tale appears in Joseph Jacobs's *Celtic Folk and Fairy Tales* (New York: G.P. Putnam, n.d.), 34–37 and has been reprinted in several children's collections (MacDonald cites four). In Jacob's Irish version a well spirit advises sprinkling objects with the water in which a child's feet have been washed. This prevents objects from opening the door when the witches return and call. They have been lured away by shouting, "The mountain of the Fenin women is on fire," and rush to Slievenamon, which Jacobs tell us is a fairy palace in Tipperary. The witches speak to the woman in Gaelic. In this tale, a rich woman had been setting up late at night carding wool when she heard the knock. She had not been complaining, and the intent of the witches, who knock and enter one by one until twelve are assembled, each with one horn more than the former, is clearly evil. Jacobs, writing in the late 1890s, cites four earlier versions from both Scotland and Ireland, most of which seem to be the milder, fairy-helpers version.

In adapting the story for my use, I introduced the tasks today's child might have to do at home—making the bed, doing dishes, sweeping the floor. I omit the sleeping husband. And at one telling, when I wanted the tale to last longer, I introduced the "change places" motif, which I liked so much that I kept.

What a Wonderful Life!
Retold from Jewish Folk Tradition

There once was an old man and an old woman who lived so happily
in a little cottage out on the edge of town.
It was so peaceful and quiet there.

Every evening the old man would stretch back in his chair and sigh,
        "What a wonderful life!"

Every evening the old woman would settle into her rocker and knit.

One evening the old man noticed...
the old woman's chair was squeaking every time she rocked.
        an-ann...an-ann...an-ann...

At first it had seemed like a small sound.
        An-ann...an-ann...an-ann...
But now that he had noticed it,
it was driving him crazy!
        *An-*ANN*...an-*ANN*...an-*ANN*...*

Then he noticed...
the old woman's knitting needles were *clicking* constantly.
        clickety-clickety-clickety-clickety...
At first it had seemed like a tiny sound.
        Clickety-clickety-clickety-clickety...
But now that he noticed it,
it was driving him crazy!
        CLICKETY-CLICKETY-CLICKETY-CLICKETY...

And *then* he noticed...
the little old woman was *humming* every time she rocked.
        Hmm-hmm...hmm-hmm...hmm-hmm...hmm-hmm...
At first it seemed like a very small sound.
        Hmm-hmm...hmm-hmm...hmm-hmm...hmm-hmm...

But now that he noticed it,
it was driving him *crazy*!
        HMM-HMM…HMM-HMM…HMM-HMM…HMM-HMM…

It never *stopped*.
        AN-ANNN…AN-ANNN…
        AN-ANNN…AN-ANNN…
        CLICKETY-CLICKETY…CLICKETY-CLICKETY…
        CLICKETY-CLICKETY…CLICKETY-CLICKETY…
        HMM-HMMM…HMM-HMMM…
        HMM-HMMM…HMM-HMMM…

The old man ran out of the house!
        "What a *horrible* life!
        Not a moment's peace and quiet in my house!"

He ran all the way to the village wise man.
        "What can I do?
        I have a horrible life!
        There is not a moment's peace and quiet in my house.
        The rocker squeaks.
        Ahn-AHN…*Ahn*-AHN…
        The knitting needles click.
        CLICKETY-CLICKETY…
        CLICKETY-CLICKETY…
        My wife hums.
        HMM-HMM…HMM-HMM…
        It's driving me *crazy*!"

The wise man thought.
And he said just one thing:
        "Get a cat."

The old man got a cat.
He took it home.
Now the chair squeaked.
        Ahn-AHN. *Ahn*-AHN.
The needles clicked.
        CLICKETY-click. CLICKETY-click.
His wife hummed.
        Hmm-hmm. Hmm-hmm.
And the cat meowed.
        MEOW-MEOW! MEOW-MEOW! MEOW-MEOW!

The old man said,
     "Worse!
     It's driving me *crazy*!"

He went back to the wise man.
     "There is no peace and quiet in my house!
     Now the chair squeaks,
     the needles click,
     my wife hums,
     and the cat meows.
     What a horrible life!"

The wise man thought.
He said just one thing.
     "Get a dog."

The old man got a dog.

Now the chair squeaked.
     *Ahn-*AHN. *Ahn-*AHN.
The needles clicked.
     CLICKETY-CLICK. CLICKETY-CLICK.
His wife hummed.
     Hmm-hmm. Hmm-hmm.
The cat meowed.
     MEOW-MEOW! MEOW-MEOW! MEOW-MEOW!
And the dog *barked*!
     WOOF-WOOF! WOOF-WOOF! WOOF-WOOF! WOOF-WOOF!

The old man said,
     "Worse and worse!
     It's driving me crazy!"

He went back to the wise man.
     "There is no peace and quiet in my house!
     The chair squeaks,
     the needles click,
     my wife hums,
     the cat meows,
     the dog barks.
     What a horrible life!"

The wise man said just one thing:
    "Get a rooster."

The old man got a rooster.

Now the chair squeaked.
    *Ahn-*AHN. *Ahn-*AHN.
The needles clicked.
    CLICKETY-CLICK. CLICKETY-CLICK.
His wife hummed.
    Hmm-hmm. Hmm-hmm.
The cat meowed.
    MEOW-MEOW! MEOW-MEOW!
The dog barked.
    WOOF-WOOF! WOOF-WOOF!
And the rooster *crowed!*
    COCK-A-DOODLE-DOO! COCK-A-DOODLE-DOO!

The old man said,
    "Worse and worse and *worse!*
    It's driving me *crazy!*"

He went back to the wise man.
    "There is no peace and quiet in my house!
    The chair squeaks,
    the needles click,
    my wife hums,
    the cat meows,
    the dog barks,
    the rooster crows.
    What a horrible life!"

The wise man said just one thing.
    "Get a goat."

The old man got a goat.

Now the chair squeaked.
    *Ahn-*AHN. *Ahn-*AHN.
The needles clicked.
    CLICKETY-CLICK. CLICKETY-CLICK.
His wife hummed.
    Hmm-hmm. Hmm-hmm.

The cat meowed.

>Meow-meow! meow-meow!

The dog barked.

>Woof-woof! woof-woof!

The rooster crowed.

>Cock-a-doodle-doo! cock-a-doodle-doo!

And the goat *bleated!*

>Baa! baa! baa! baa!

The old man said,

>"Worse and worse and worse and *worse!*"
>It's driving me *crazy!*"

He went back to the wise man.

>"There is no peace and quiet in my house!
>The chair squeaks,
>the needles click,
>my wife hums,
>the cat meows,
>the dog barks,
>the rooster crows,
>the goat bleats.
>What a horrible life!"

The wise man said just one thing:

>"Get a cow."

The old man got a cow.

Now the chair squeaked.

>*Ahn-*AHN. *Ahn-*AHN.

The needles clicked.

>Clickety-click. clickety-click.

His wife hummed.

>*Hmm-hmm. Hmm-hmm.*

The cat meowed.

>Meow-meow! meow-meow!

The dog barked.

>Woof-woof! woof-woof!

The rooster crowed.

>Cock-a-doodle-doo! cock-a-doodle-doo!

The goat bleated.
      BAA! BAA! BAA! BAA!
And the cow *mooed!*
      MOO! MOO! MOO! MOO!

The old man said,
      "Worse and worse and *worst of all*!
      It's driving me crazy!"

He went back to the wise man.
      "There is no peace and quiet in my house.
      The chair squeaks,
      the needles click,
      my wife hums,
      the cat meows,
      the dog barks,
      the rooster crows,
      the goat bleats,
      the cow moos.
      What a horrible life!
      This is worst of *all*!"

      "Ah," said the wise man.
      "I can help."
The wise man said just five things:
      "Take back the cow.
      Take back the goat.
      Take back the rooster.
      Take back the dog.
      Take back the cat."

The old man took back the cow.
He took back the goat.
He took back the rooster.
He took back the dog.
He took back the cat.

He went back home.
He sat in his chair.
The rocker creaked,
      ann-ann...ann-ann...

The needles clicked,
>*clickety-clickety…*
>*clickety-clickety…*

His good wife hummed,
>*hmm-hmmm…hmm-hmmm…*

It was *so* peaceful.

He stretched back in his chair and sighed.

>"Such peace and quiet in my house,
>What a wonderful life…
>What a wonderful life!"

Tips for telling:

Of course, the audience is encouraged to join in on all of the noises. Sometimes I let each person select the sound they wish to make; at other times, I divide the audience into groups to produce each sound. And it can be fun to bring up a few audience members to act the parts of the rocking, knitting, humming, meowing, barking, crowing, bleating, and mooing. If you like, each can lead their own humming, clicking, mooing section of the audience. Each time a new animal is added, you should go through the whole rigmarole again.

About the story:

MacDonald Motif *Z49.16* Man complaining of too much noise procures additional animals as remedy.* This cites Yiddish and Ukrainian versions of the tale. Z49.16 has been retold in picture-book format several times and is a favorite of storytellers. An especially tellable picture book version is *Too Much Noise* by Ann McGovern, illustrated by Simms Taback (Boston: Houghton Mifflin, 1967), and an excellent audio telling is Syd Lieberman's "The Noisy House" in *Joseph the Tailor and Other Jewish Tales* (Little Rock: August House, 1988).

9 Tandem Telling

MANY STORIES BREAK EASILY INTO TWO PARTS. THESE can be used for two tellers, or two groups of participants. You can use such tandem tales in several ways.

1. *Group participation*: Break the group into two halves. Before you begin telling assign a character to each half of the audience. Then, as you tell, let the audience halves participate in their character's songs or chants. I often use this technique when telling "The Gunnywolf." This is the story of Little Girl accosted by the Gunnywolf. Sometimes I pass out crepe paper flowers to those playing "Little Girl" and crepe paper tails to those playing the "Gunnywolf." The Gunnywolves shake their tails as they hunkercha and roar. With or without the props, the "Little Girl" half of the audience sings along with the "cum-kwa-ki-wa" song as Little Girl picks flowers. The "Gunnywolf" half of the audience slap their legs and "hunkercha" as the gunnywolf gallops after to catch her.

2. *Acting it out in two groups*: First tell the story. Now break the group into two halves, sending one to one side of the room and one to the other. Retell the story, letting the two sides act out their characters.

With my preschool groups, I enjoy using this technique for the story "Grandfather Bear is Hungry." In this story, Grandfather Bear wakes up hungry and goes foraging for berries or fish. Finally Chipmunk offers him nuts. I divide the group into bears and chipmunks. All of the bears lumber about with me. All of the chipmunks gather their food. It helps to have a second adult to guide one of the groups when doing this tandem work with many small children.

3. *Partners act as you tell*: Tell the story. Then have each person choose a partner. They must decide who will play each role. As you retell the story, each member acts out the role. For example, when playing "Grandfather Bear," one person in each pair will play the part of the Bear; the other person is Chipmunk.

4. *Partner telling*: Tell the story. Let partners retell the story and act it out on their own. One person takes each roll. You will need to

demonstrate this first with a volunteer. Just tell a bit of the story, showing how tandem telling can be used. This is a useful technique for teaching stories to storytelling students, either adults or children.

I often work with older children, preparing them to perform for younger classrooms. In working with these groups, I suggest that they use a "story theatre" format. In this format, the teller/actor *tells* the story while acting it out. Grandfather Bear says: "Grandfather Bear woke up one fine spring morning. He came out of his cave. He was *so* hungry. Grandfather Bear said, 'I am *so* hungry!'" The teller acts this out as he tells. But the teller continues to keep also the role of story-teller, describing the action as he acts it. This technique is a little hard to teach but makes for an effective performance once it becomes second nature. See the chapter on "Story Theatre" for more on this technique.

5. *Parent-child participation*: Parents assume one role, children the other. You retell as they act out the story. When working with parent-child groupings (common in my preschool storytime programs at the public library), I assign one role to the parent, the other to that parent's children. Then I retell, and the parents and children follow along with my actions and vocalizations. I love using this technique with a story about "Elk and Wren." In this story, wren is singing and elk is trying to sleep. With my preschool storytime groups I tell the story once, letting the children all chime in on the wren's song. Then I ask the group to stand and form a circle. We put all of the children in the middle of the circle and the adults (moms, grandmas, dads, etc.) form the ring. The children are wrens and dance about, singing. The adults are elks. The elks keep telling the wrens to stop singing so they can sleep, and the wrens sass the elks back. I, of course, simply retell the story, giving both parts their cue.

6. *Performing with a friend*: You might have fun performing a tandem tale with a friend. It requires a bit of rehearsal, but is worth the effort. This sort of telling can add a lively spot to your program. Children's librarians who team in branches often have fun with this sort of tandem telling.

Most tales with two characters will work in this tandem-telling format. Below is a list of suggested tales. Two stories, "The Elephants and the Bees" and "Little Boy Frog and Little Boy Snake," are included to get you started.

Tales with tandem possibilities:

"Elk and Wren" in *Look Back and See* by Margaret Read MacDonald (New York: H.W. Wilson, 1991),103–6. Elk is annoyed at wren's singing. Nice interplay between the two characters, grumpy elk and sassy, singing wren.

"Hen and Frog" in *Beat the Story Drum, Pum-Pum* by Ashley Bryan (New York: Atheneum, 1980). Frog lazes while hen works. Hear Ashley's rendition on *The Dancing Granny and other African Stories* (New York: Caedmon, 1989).

"Why Koala Has No Tail" from *Look Back and See* by Margaret Read MacDonald (New York: H.W. Wilson, 1991), 74–80. This tandem tale makes a fun performance piece for children. One child is koala, the other is tree kangaroo. Each tells about the character's actions as it is acted. A narrator can also be used in this piece if the children want to work in threes. The narrator can introduce the story and lead the audience in participation. Tree Kangaroo digs a lot, and it is fun to have the audience dig along with him.

"Grandfather Bear is Hungry" from *Look Back and See* by Margaret Read MacDonald (New York: H.W. Wilson, 1991), 126–29. This is a very easy tandem piece with which beginners can always achieve success. One person is Chipmunk, the other Grandfather Bear. Grandfather Bear has most of the lines as he describes his waking up in the spring, looking for berries and salmon, and finally scraping at a stump. Chipmunk (who has been crouching under the stump) now jumps up and enters the action, offering Grandfather Bear nuts. The story ends very sweetly as Grandfather Bear pulls his claw softly down chipmunk's back, leaving five black stripes. It creates a gentle moment in our storytime as bears all give their chipmunks a soft stroke on the back.

"The Gunny Wolf" in *Twenty Tellable Tales* by Margaret Read MacDonald (New York: H.W. Wilson, 1986), 68–74, or in picture book *The Gunniwolf* by Wilhelmina Harper, illus. by William Wiesner (New York: Dutton, 1967).

"How to Break a Bad Habit" in *Twenty Tellable Tales* by Margaret Read MacDonald (New York: H.W. Wilson, 1986), 79–89. Monkey scratches, rabbit twitches. Each tries to stop. Lots of active possibilities here.

"The Pancake" in *Just Enough to Make a Story* by Nancy Schimmel (Berkeley: Sisters Choice, 1982), 24–25. Formatted by Gay Ducey and Nancy Schimmel for tandem performance.

"Pickin' Peas," see page 61, and in picture book *Pickin' Peas* by Margaret Read MacDonald, illus. by Pat Cummings (New York: HarperCollins, 1998).

Tandem Tellers on Tape:

Cockroach Party! Folktales to Sing, Dance & Act Out told by Margaret Read MacDonald, music by Richard Scholtz. (Bellingham, Wash.: Live Music Recordings, 1999). "Teeny Weeny Bop."

The Folktellers: Tales to Grow On told by Connie Regan and Barbara Freeman (Weston, Conn.: Weston Woods, 1982). Listen to "The King at the Door."

World Tales: Live at Bennington College told by Tim Jennings and Leanne Ponder (Burlington, VT: Eastern Coyote Productions, 1997). Skillful use of the tandem form on all tales.

The Elephants and the Bees
A Folktale from Thailand

Once a fire raged through the forest.
The elephants were terrified.
They did not know which way to go to escape.

Just then a cloud of bees buzzed over their heads.
> "Bees! Bees!
> Help us escape!
> You can fly high in the air and see the flames.
> Tell us which way to go!"

> *"Bzzzz…Bzzzz…*Sure. We'll help you."

The bees flew high into the air.
They looked to the east.
Fire!
They looked to the west.
Fire!
They looked to the south.
Fire!
They looked to the north.
There was a river!
The elephants could be safe there.

> "Come on, elephants.
> We will lead you to safety.
> Follow us!"

And they led the way.
> *"Bzzzzzzzzz…"*
Up the hill.
> *"Bzzzzzzzz…"*

Down the hill.
    "Bzzzzzzz…"
Right to the river!

    "Wade on in, elephants!
    You will be safe here!"

The elephants waded into the deep water.
Only the tips of their little noses were showing.
In those days, the elephants had short, short noses
like a pig!

Just then the flames came over the hilltop.
The smoke began to billow down the hill.

    "Help! Help!" buzzed the bees.
    "This smoke will kill *us*!
    We saved *you*, elephants.
    Now you must save *us*.
    Open your mouths!
    Open your mouths and let us come inside.
    We will be safe from the smoke!"

    "What?
    Open our mouths?"
But the elephants had to repay the bees.
So they opened their mouths wide.
    "Bzzzzzzz…"
The bees all went inside the elephant's heads.
The elephants closed their mouths.
Now their heads sounded like *"bzzzzzzzzzzz…"*
But they kept their mouths shut to save the bees.
The flames roared down the hill.
The flames *jumped* the river
and roared up the other hill and away.

When the smoke had cleared away
the elephants opened their mouths.
    "Okay bees! You can come out now."

    *"Bzzzzzzz…*we *like* it in here," said the bees.
    "It is nice and warm and moist and dark.
    We are going to stay here and make honey!"

The elephant's heads were going *"Bzzzzzzz…"*
They thought they would go crazy!

"We *have* to get those bees out.
What will we do?"

"I know! We can *wash* them out!"

"Good idea!"

The elephants each took a *big* mouthful of water.
They *blew* it out their *noses*!
"Prae Pren!
Prae Pren!
Prae Pren!"

It didn't work.

"Try harder, elephants!"

"Prae Pren!
Prae Pren!
Prae Pren!"

"It isn't working!
Blow *harder*!"

"Prae Pren!
Prae Pren!
Prae Pren!"

"*Stop stop*!
Look what is happening to our *noses*!"

Every time the elephants blew…
their noses got a little longer!
Now they were almost touching the ground!

"This isn't working.
We have to think of something else.
The bees were afraid of smoke.
Maybe we could *smoke* them out."

The elephants built a little smoky fire.

Each took a deep breath of the smoke.
They *held* their breath.

It worked!
Those bees couldn't stand that smoke.
They flew right out of the elephant's long noses.

> *"Bzzzzzzz…"*

But the bees had really liked living inside the elephant's heads.
So to this day they make their homes
inside hollow trees in the forest.
They look for a dark hole shaped just like
the inside of an elephant's head.
They are called Phung Phrong bees, bees who live in a hole like
an elephant's head.

And the elephants…
sometimes they feel as if bees are *still* crawling around
inside their heads.
When that happens, they just suck up lots of water
and squirt it out their noses
to *wash out all the bees*!

So if you see an elephant squirting water around,
tell him,

> "Don't worry, Mr. Elephant.
> The bees are all gone.
> The bees are all gone."

Tips for telling:

It is fun to encourage your audience to buzz along with the bees. When the elephants squirt water, let your audience pretend to wave trunks and shout, "Prae Pren!" When Wajuppa Tossa tells this story, she asks each child in the audience to put their hand on the shoulder of a neighbor and pat them gently, saying, "Don't worry. The bees are all gone." This creates a very tender scene in the auditorium as the children quietly comfort each other.

When telling in tandem, the bee usually flits about, encouraging the audience to buzz along and then hides behind the elephant (after flying into its head). From there the bee pokes out from time to time to encourage the audience to keep buzzing when the bee buzzes. The elephant in turn encourages the audience to squirt water and "Prae Pren."

About the story:

This story is retold from "The Elephants and the Bees" in *Thai Tales: Folktales of Thailand* by Supaporn Vathanaprida, edited by Margaret Read MacDonald (Englewood, Colo.: Libraries Unlimited, 1994). The story was shaped by the Mahasarakham Storytelling Troupe through repeated tandem tellings, and especially by Prasong Saihong and Dr. Wajuppa Tossa. A Thai version appears in *Nithan Chaoban Khong Thai* by Yut Detkhamron (Bangkok: Khlangwitthaya, 2521 B.E.), 470–72. It includes Motif *A2335.3 Origin and nature of animal's proboscis* and *B481.3 Helpful bees*.

Little Boy Frog and Little Boy Snake

Based on an Ekoi Folktale

As retold by Jim Wolf.

Little Boy Frog asked his Momma,
　　　"May I go out and play?"

　　　"Go play," said his Momma.
　　　"But be careful where you go.
　　　Don't talk to strangers.
　　　And don't play too late."

So Little Boy Frog went out.
　　　Hop…hop…hop…hop…

Little Boy Snake asked his Momma,
　　　"May I go out and play?"

　　　"Yes, you may," said his Momma.
　　　"But be careful where you go.
　　　Don't talk to strangers.
　　　And don't play too late."

So Little Boy Snake went out.
　　　Slide…slide…slide…slide…

　　　Hop…hop…hop…hop…

　　　Slide…slide…slide…slide…

　　　"Oh! Who are you?"

　　　"I'm Little Boy Frog.
　　　Who are you?"

"I'm Little Boy Snake."

"Want to play?"

"Sure!"

So Little Boy Snake and Little Boy Frog began to play together.

Little Boy Snake slid.
Little Boy Frog hopped.

"What's that you are doing?" asked Little Boy Snake.

"I am hopping!"

"How do you do that?"

So Little Boy Frog showed Little Boy Snake how to hop.

Hop…hop…hop…hop…

The two friends played together.

"What's that *you* were doing?" asked Little Boy Frog.

"Oh, I was sliding."

"Can you show me how?"

So Little Boy Snake showed Little Boy Frog how to slide.

The two friends played together.
Slide…slide…slide…slide…

"This was fun!
Want to play again tomorrow?"

"Okay! See you tomorrow!"

And the two friends went home.

Little Boy Frog could *slide*.
Hop…slide…hop…slide…

Little Boy Snake could *hop*.
>   *Slide…hop…slide…hop…*

Little Boy Frog came home.
>   *Hop…slide…hop…slide…*

Momma Frog saw her son coming.
>   "What's that you are doing?

>   "I am *sliding*!
>   My friend taught me how. Watch!"
>   *Slide…slide…slide…*

>   "*Stop*! What kind of friend was *that*?"

>   "His name was Little Boy Snake."

>   "Oh no, no, no, my son.
>   The snakes are our *enemies*.
>   You must *never* play with a *snake*."

Little Boy Snake went home.
>   *Slide…hop…slide…hop…*

His Momma saw him coming.
>   "What are you doing, son?"

>   "I am *hopping*!"
>   My friend taught me how. Watch!"
>   *Hop…hop…hop…*

>   "*Stop*! What kind of friend was *that*?"

>   "His name was Little Boy Frog."

>   "Oh no, no, no, my son.
>   The frogs are our *food*.
>   You must *never* play with a *frog*.
>   Now go to bed."

Next day Little Boy Frog went out to play.
Little Boy Snake went out to play.
They met each other.

"I can't play with you anymore,"
said Little Boy Frog.
"You are our enemy."

"I can't play with you anymore either,"
said Little Boy Snake.
"You are our food."

The two friends turned and went away.
Hop…hop…hop…
Slide…slide…slide…

But before they were completely out of sight,
they turned to look back at each other one more time.
And then…

Little Boy Frog moved
hop…slide…hop…slide…

Little Boy Snake moved
slide…hop…slide…hop…

They laughed!

Then Little Boy Frog went on home.
Hop…SLIDE…*hop*…SLIDE!

And little Boy Snake went on home.
Slide…HOP…*slide*…HOP!

Their Mommas wouldn't let them *play* together.
But they could still remember.

Tips for telling:

Use one swaying arm to represent the sliding snake, the other
hopping hand to represent the frog. Of course soon each is both
hopping *and* sliding. The children will join you in these arm motions,
which quietly trail off at the story's end as the two friends disappear in
opposite directions.

About the story:

This telling is based on the story as told by Jim Wolf, of Boone,
North Carolina. I heard Jim perform this many times during two

months of touring in Northeastern Thailand in the winter of 1997. He told the story in tandem with Prasong Saihong, who repeated each phrase in Lao for our non-English-speaking audience. The two moved about the stage a great deal as they told, encouraging the school audiences to join in arm motions as frog and snake hopped and slid. This Ekoi story was published by P. Amaury Talbot in *In the Shadow of the Bush* (London: Heinemann,1912), 386, as a brief eighteen-line tale. Ashley Bryan elaborated this into a wonderful eleven-page story, "Why Frog and Snake Never Play Together" in *Beat the Story-Drum, Pum-Pum* (New York: Atheneum, 1980), 41–52. Ashley Bryan adds a good bit of his inimitable word play and introduces a chant to the story. William J. Bennet retells Bryan's tale in briefer and blander form in his *Children's Book of Virtues* (New York: Simon & Schuster, 1995). Bryan introduced the notion of picking up each other's gait. He kept the Talbot ending in which the Snake Child appears to be planning to eat Frog Child on their second meeting. The line is "Evidently our mother has given you instructions. My mother also has given me instructions." So the two part and sit alone forevermore. Our ending, in which each is altered by their brief friendship, seems an invention of Jim Wolf.

Motif *A2441.4 Cause of movement of reptile.* MacDonald/Sturm *A2441.4.6ª Frog learns to slide from snake. Snake learns to hop from frog.*

10 Story Theatre

STORY THEATRE IS A TECHNIQUE IN WHICH THE ACTORS both tell *and* act out the story. At no time do the actors drop the voice of the storyteller. For example, the teller playing Pán Kotsky (p. 147) might say, "Pán Kotsky was a very proud cat. He proudly called himself, 'Pán Kotsky!'" The teller acts the part of Pán Kotsky, strutting about the stage and delivering the lines "Pán Kotsky!" in character. The teller thus *acts* as he tells. Or, conversely, we could say that the actor *tells* as he acts. As more characters enter, they also act and speak their own lines while telling about the actions of their characters. The presentation might go something like this.

TELLER #1 *(playing Pán Kotsky):*

Pán Kotsky dressed like a gentleman at all times.
When he went out, how he did strut.
He made everyone call him…"Pán Kotsky!"
One day Pán Kotsky went for a stroll in the forest.

TELLER #2 *(playing Little Fox):*

There he met the sweetest little lady fox.
Little Fox looked at Pán Kotsky.
> "My, but you are beautiful, sir!
> What kind of animal are you?
> I have never seen an animal like you in these woods."

TELLER #1:

Pán Kotsky began to strut back and forth.
> "I am the most fierce and famous creature in this forest.
> Don't tell me you have never heard of…Pán Kotsky!"

This can be an enjoyable technique to use when telling with a friend. It can also be a creative way to help students prepare a story performance. Each summer, I offer a storytelling workshop for elementary students at my library. We meet for three weeks, learn a few stories, rehearse, and in the fourth week perform for parents and the general public. The children manage to do engaging performances using tandem-telling techniques and story theatre. I also use this technique in my story play workshops for adults as a lively way to fasten the story onto my students. Story theatre works especially well to wake up workshop participants in late afternoon.

Many stories can be adapted to play well in this format. Look for tales with distinctive characters, straightforward plot, and simple dialogue. The story theatre technique works easily with stories from the "Tandem Telling" section (p. 131).

This technique was perfected by Paul Sills and his Story Theatre troupe during the early Seventies. I was fortunate to see them at Kennedy Center, and we never missed their television series during the winter of 1971–72. To see the elaborate scripting techniques used by Paul Sills for his productions, consult *Story Theatre: Adapted for the stage by Paul Sills from Stories in the Grimm Brothers' Collection and Aesop's Fables* (New York: Samuel French, 1971) and *More from Story Theatre* by Paul Sills (New York: Samuel French, 1981). These scripts require royalties for performance, but from them you might discover ways to treat your own tale material using this format.

Suggested tales for story theatre format:

Anansi and the Moss-Covered Rock retold by Eric A. Kimmel, illus. by Janet Stevens (New York: Holiday House, 1988).

"Biyera Well" in *Look Back and See* by Margaret Read MacDonald (New York: H.W. Wilson, 1991), 90–94. Delightful Egyptian tale of three animals who farm together. To discover who has been eating up the clover, they must each jump over the well. Good as story theatre or fun for the whole group to act out afterwards.

Fin M'Coul: The Giant of Knockmanyhill by Tomie de Paola (New York: Holiday House, 1981).

Half-a-Ball-of-Kenki by Verna Aardema, illus. by Diane Stanley (New York: Frederick Warne, 1979). Also in *Misoso: Once Upon a Time Tales from Africa* by Verna Aardema (New York: Knopf, 1994).

"Little Thumb Conquers the Sun" in *The Oryx Multicultural Folktale Series: Tom Thumb* by Margaret Read MacDonald (Phoenix, Ariz.: Oryx, 1993), 102–9.

Who's in Rabbit's House by Verna Aardema, illus. by Leo and Diane Dillon (New York: Dial, 1977).

Pán Kotsky

A Folktale from the Ukraine

Pán Kotsky was a cat.
But such a *proud* cat.
Pán Kotsky dressed like a gentleman at all times.
When he went out, how he did strut.

One day Pán Kotsky went for a stroll in the forest.
And there he met the sweetest little lady fox.

Little Fox looked at Pán Kotsky.
> "My, but you are beautiful, sir!
> What kind of animal are you?
> I have never seen an animal like you in these woods."

Pán Kotsky began to strut back and forth.
> "I am the most fierce and famous creature in this forest.
> Don't tell me you have never heard of Pán Kotsky!"

Little Fox was much impressed.
She fell straightaway in love with this vain creature.

> "Oh, but won't you come home and visit me?" she asked.
> "I am small and nervous.
> I would love to have a fierce and famous creature at
>   my house."

Pán Kotsky gladly accepted.
In fact, he made himself quite comfortable in the little fox's home.
Each day Little Fox went out to find something for their dinner.
And each evening she came back to prepare food for Pán Kotsky.
He had no reason ever to stir himself.

One day, as Little Fox was out running errands,
she ran into Mr. Rabbit.

"Dear Little Fox," said Mr. Rabbit.
"I was hoping to meet you.
Might I come courting you one day soon?"

"I think *not*!" said Little Fox.
"I already *have* a handsome caller at my house.
His name is Pán Kotsky!
And he is the most fierce and famous creature in the
      forest."

Mr. Rabbit went away quite disappointed.

Next day, as Little Fox was out doing errands,
she met Mr. Boar.

"Good day, Little Fox!" said Mr. Boar.
I was hoping to meet you.
Might I come courting one day soon?"

"I should think *not*!" exclaimed Little Fox.
"I already *have* a handsome caller at my house.
His name is Pán Kotsky!
And he is the most fierce and famous creature in the
      forest."

Mr. Boar left in great unhappiness.

The next day, who should Little Fox meet in the forest but Mr. Bear?

"Little Fox! I am so glad I ran into you.
Would you let me come courting some day soon?"

"No I would *not*!
I already *have* a handsome caller at my house.
His name is Pán Kotsky!
He is the most fierce and famous creature in the forest."

So Mr. Bear too went away sad.

Bear and Boar and Rabbit were curious to see this new creature.
"Why don't we invite Little Fox and this Pán Kotsky to
      dinner?
Then we can see how 'fierce and famous' this
      character really is."

They sent Rabbit to deliver the invitation.
      "We would love to come," said Little Fox.
And before Pán Kotsky could poke his head out the door,
Rabbit rushed away.
He didn't feel up to meeting Pán Kotsky alone.

When the evening of the dinner came,
the animals prepared a fine feast.
As the hour for the arrival of Pán Kotsky drew near,
they became increasingly nervous.

      "I just had an idea," said Mr. Bear.
      "I think I will wait up in the oak tree.
      That way I can see Pán Kotsky before he sees *me*."

      "Good idea," said Mr. Boar.
      "I believe I will just lie under the table here
      out of sight.
      That way I can see Pán Kotsky before he sees *me*."

      "Yes, Yes," agreed Mr. Rabbit.
      "And I will lie behind this log.
      That way I can see Pán Kotsky before he sees *me*."

So the animals hid.

Soon in came Little Fox with her Pán Kotsky.
As soon as that cat saw the table laden with food,
he *jumped* right into the middle of it and began to gobble the
    goodies.
And when dear Little Fox reached for a bite…
      "Myarr! myarr! myarr!" he snarled.

The hiding animals thought he was shouting for "*More! more! more!*"

In the tree, Bear was trembling.
Behind the log, Rabbit's teeth were chattering.
And under the table,
Boar was so nervous that his tail began to swish.
Back…and forth…back…and forth…

Pán Kotsky saw that tail moving.
He mistook it for a *mouse*.

And being a *cat*…
Pán Kotsky *pounced* on the end of Boar's tail with a
        "Raawwwrrrr!"
And bit as hard as he could.

Boar jumped up. *"Aaaahhh!"*
He knocked over the table,
and ran blindly away so fast that he smashed into the oak tree.

When Boar whunked into the oak tree,
Bear was jolted from his perch,
and fell squash onto poor Rabbit's back!

Rabbit ran off calling, "Help! Help! Help!"
with Bear and Boar right behind.

The three animals gathered trembling in the forest.

      "Did you see what he *did*?" said Boar.
      "Pán Kotsky bit off my tail!"

      "That's nothing," said Bear.
      "Pán Kotsky knocked me out of the tree!"

      "Even worse," said Rabbit,
      "He whacked *me* on the back with a huge club.
      I am black and blue all over."

The animals vowed never to go near the fierce and famous Pán
   Kotsky again.

And as for Pán Kotsky?
When a boar leaped up from under the table, he had nearly died
   of fright.
Next, a huge bear jumped down from the tree.
And a rabbit raced off screaming, "Help! Help!" for others to
   come attack.
Pán Kotsky climbed the oak tree as fast as he could and clung
   there trembling.

Little Fox took a long look at her fierce and famous gentleman
   caller.
She looked at the three animals trembling in the woods.

Little Fox shook her head in disgust.

"No more gentlemen callers," she said.

And she went home and locked her door.

He who talks big
does not always act big.

Tips for telling:

From the very first time I mention Pán Kotsky, I always pause before saying his name and then pronounce it with a great flourish. Soon the audience will join in. In performing the story as story theatre, the same trick may be used, but in this format you might want to make a thing of having Pán Kotsky ask the audience to repeat his name when he is first introduced to the story.

About the story:

Retold from "Pán Kotsky" in *Ukrainian Folk Tales* by Marie Halun Block, illustrated by J. Hnizdovsky (New York: Coward-McCann, 1964), 24–27. Translated from the Original Collections of Ivan Rudchenko and Maria Lukiyanenko. Another variant is found as *Mister Cat-and-a-half* by Richard Peucar, illustrated by Robert Rayesky (New York: Macmillan, 1986).

This is Motif *K2324 Hiding from strange animal. A cat shrieks and the frightened bear falls out of the tree and hurts himself. Cat as husband of she-fox has been invited to feast by animals, they hide and cat pounces on boar's ear, wolf's nose, etc. thinking it is mouse. In ensuing ruckus bear falls and hiding animals flee. Types 103 The Wild Animals Hide from the Unfamiliar Animal; 103A The Cat as She-Fox's Husband.* MacDonald cites variants from Russia, Latvia, Finland, Poland, and Germany.

Nanny Goat and Her Two Little Kids

A Folktale from France

When Nanny Goat had to leave her children
she always warned them:
        "Don't open the door for anyone while I am gone."
When she came back, Nanny Goat would knock three times.
        RAP! RAP! RAP!
She would sing out in her sweet mother's voice,
        "Little he kid…little she kid…
        Open the door.
        It's your mother!"
Then Nanny Goat would lean over
and poke her leg through the little cat door.
When the children saw that white, white leg,
they would know it was their mother.
            "Now jump up!
            As if straw were tickling your bottoms!
            And open this door!"
Those kids would jump up and open the door!
How they would hug their mother!

One day Nanny Goat had to go off to St. Jard.
As she left she called back to them,
        "While I am gone stay safe in the house.
        And don't open the door for *anyone*
        until you hear me call
        'Little he kid…little she kid…
        Open the door!
        It's your mother!'"

Unfortunately…
a wolf was hanging about in the forest nearby.

He heard everything the mother said.
　　　"This is luck for *me*!" thought the wolf.
He walked right up to the little kids' house.
He knocked three times on the door.
　　　RAP! RAP! RAP!
Then he sang out in his best wolf voice,
　　　"Little he kid…little she kid…
　　　Open the door!
　　　It's your mother!"

　　　"Who is that singing?
　　　That's not our mother.
　　　You're the *wolf*!
　　　Go away! Go away! Go away!"

The wolf went away.
But he didn't stay away.

　　　"I can sing like their mother.
　　　It just takes a little practice."

So the wolf practiced.
　　　"Little he kid…little she kid…
And he practiced.
　　　"Little he kid…little she kid…"
And he practiced.
　　　"Little he kid…little she kid…
　　　Open the door!"
Till he got it right.
　　　"Little he kid…little she kid…
　　　Open the door!
　　　It's your mother!"

He sang so sweetly.
He sounded just like their mother.

Back went the wolf.
　　　RAP! RAP! RAP!

　　　"Little he kid…little she kid…
　　　Open the door…
　　　It's your mother!"

"Oh! Our mother is home already!"
The kids ran to the door.
"No, wait. We didn't see her white, white leg.
Show us your leg.
The wolf has been trying to trick us.
Poke your leg in at the cat hole
so we can be sure it is you."
The wolf bent over and poked his leg in the cat hole.
But the wolf's leg was brown and furry.

"That isn't our mother's leg.
Our mother's leg is white and smooth.
You're the *wolf*!
Go away! Go away! Go away!"

The wolf went away.
But he didn't stay away.
"They want to see a white leg.
I can fix that."
The wolf went home and stuck his leg in the flour bin.
He rubbed and rubbed
until the leg looked smooth and white.

RAP! RAP! RAP!
"Little he kid…little she kid…
Open the door.
It's your mother!"

"Show us your leg.
The wolf has been trying to trick us."

The wolf poked his white, smooth leg in the cat door.

"Oh mother, you're home!"
The kids threw open the door.
"*The wolf!*"

"Yes, the *wolf*. And I am *hungry*!
Feed me quick or I will eat you *both*."

"We have cakes…
do you want cakes?
Our mother baked cakes this morning."

"I want cakes."

"They are cooling in the bread bin."

That wolf jumped into the bread bin.
He began to devour cakes.
     "Mmmm...mmmm...mmmm..."
Slowly the kids closed the lid of the bread bin.
The wolf didn't even notice.
     "Mmmmm...mmmm...mmmm..."

Thank goodness, a knock at the door.
     RAP! RAP! RAP!
     "Little he kid...little she kid...
     Open the door...
     It's your mother!"

     "Oh Mama, you're back!...
     Show us your leg...
     Yes! It's really you!"

     "Jump up!
     As if straw were tickling your bottoms.
     And open the door!" sang their mother.

How glad they were to see their Mama.
     "The *wolf* has been here!"

     "What?"

     "He's *still here*!"

     "Where?"

     "In the bread bin, eating your cakes.
     We closed the lid."

     "Good thinking.
     Now go sit on the lid so he can't get out.
     I will get busy and boil some water."

Soon the wolf finished eating the cakes.
     "Mmm...mmm...mmm..."

But when he tried to get out
he bumped his head on the lid.
> "Ouch! Open this lid!"

> "Just a moment…" called Nanny Goat.
> "I'm coming…"

She carried the pot of boiling water to the bread bin
and began to pour the scalding water down between the cracks.

> *Sssss*…"OUCH!"
> *Sssss*…"OUCH!"
> *Sssss*…"OUCH!"

The wolf twisted and turned, trying to escape.
> "Let me out! Let me out!"

> "If we let you out, will you go away?"

> *Sssss*…"OUCH! Yes, I'll go away!"

> "And will you stay away?"

> *Sssss*…"OUCH! Yes, I'll stay away!"

> "Jump aside, children. We will let him go."

Nanny Goat lifted the lid
and that wolf *hurled* himself out the front door.
Way over the fields he ran.

Nanny Goat ran to the threshold and called after him,
> "The runnning wolf is on the way!
> Look out, shepherdess in the hay!
> The scalded wolf is on the run!
> Look out, shepherds every one!"

That wolf ran so fast
and that wolf ran so far
that this time he never came back.

Tips for telling:

The children will enjoy singing with you on mother goat's song, "Little he kid...little she kid..." And they can knock with her too. To play it as story theatre you can always add more kids if you want to engage the whole group. After all, another story just like this had *seven* kids.

About the story:

Retold from "The Goat, the Kids, and the Wolf" in *Folktales from France* by Geneviève Massignon (Chicago: University of Chicago Press, 1968). The story was collected in 1959 from a seventy-nine-year-old woman in Montjean. This is a variant of *K311.3 Thief disguises voice and is allowed access to goods (children)*. MacDonald's *Storyteller's Sourcebook* cites variants from Germany (Grimms), Haiti, Italy, Jamaica, Korea, North Africa, Russia, U.S. (Georgia), Taiwan, Tanganyika, and Uganda.

11 Act-It-Out Tales

ONE OF MY FAVORITE WAYS TO EXTEND A STORY IS TO simply assign parts and retell the story immediately while acting it out. This can be done very simply. After telling, I ask, "Would you like to play the story?" "Who would like to be the dog?" If several raise their hands then I may have two or three playing the dog's part. This technique works especially well for stories that have a traveling hero who meets several characters en route. First I get volunteers to play the several characters the hero meets during the story. The rest of us all play the part of the hero and set out on the adventure. I use all space available in the room or yard, placing the various characters at some distance from each other. "Henny Penny," for example, would work well in this sort of story play. Assign a few geese, turkeys, a fox, and the rest of us can all be Henny Pennys. If the story does not include a refrain, you may want to think up some sort of marching chant or song to move you on your way.

With small children, I do not assign specific parts. After I tell "Pickin' Peas" (p. 61) I ask, "Who wants to be Little Girl?" "Who wants to be Mister Rabbit?" All of those who want to be Little Girl go to one side of the room. All of the rabbits go to the other. Each group walks or hops after me, echoing my actions and voice as we re-enact the story. In a preschool setting with parents on hand, I utilize the parents as characters. Thus, in "Elk and Wren," a story in which Little Wren annoys Elk with her singing, the children (wrens) dance in the middle of a circle of adults (elk). The told story involves only two characters, but in acting it out we turn it into a group play. The wrens dance and sing. The elk, who are trying to sleep, call into the circle telling the wrens to be quiet.

You may also want to try creative dramatics activities in which each child takes one role and the children act out the play. Several good manuals for this type of dramatic play are available. You might begin with those by Burdette S. Fitzgerald, Rives Collins and Pamela Cooper, and Judy Sierra.

Tales to act:

The Bossy Gallito/El Gallo de Bodas: A Traditional Cuban Folktale retold by Lucía M. González, illus. by Lulu Delacre (New York: Scholastic, 1994).

"Chicken Licken" in *Great Children's Stories: The Classic Volland Edition* written and illus. by Frederick Richardson (Chicago: Rand McNally, 1972), 81–91.

"Elk and Wren" in *Look Back and See* by Margaret Read MacDonald (New York: H.W. Wilson, 1991), 103–6.

The Gingerbread Boy by Paul Galdone (New York: Clarion, 1975).

"Going to Ceviéres" in *Celebrate the World* by Margaret Read MacDonald (New York: H.W. Wilson, 1994), 202–9. Animals travel to the mountainside spa for their health. Audience chants along.

"Jack and the Robbers" from *Twenty Tellable Tales* by Margaret Read MacDonald (New York: H.W. Wilson, 1986), 95–103. This works especially well as there is already a traveling chant in the story, "jiggelty-jolt." And there is lots of noisy activity for all players. If you are working with a small enough number of actors it is fun to stack up the animals at the end, with one's hands on the next's shoulders. This is a version of "The Bremen Town Musicians" and the animals all stack themselves up to frighten the robbers with loud crowing, barking, etc.

"Kanji-jo, the Nestlings" from *Tuck-Me-In Tales* by Margaret Read MacDonald (Little Rock: August House, 1996), 24–36. One of my favorite moments using this story was at a program for young children and seniors in my hometown library in Jennings County, Indiana. The story tells of young chicks looking for their mother. The chicks run to various mother birds calling, "Mamá! Mamá! Mamá!" The mother birds comfort them, feed them, and send them on next morning in search of their real mother. Senior ladies playing the mother birds were so delighted to be surrounded by peeping preschoolers. This is a lengthy story but well worth the time. It ends with all birds dancing and singing after they are reunited with their mother.

"Ticky Picky Boom Boom Bouf" in *Anansi the Spider Man: Jamaican Folk Tales* by Philip Sherlock (New York: Crowell, 1954), 76–83, and in *Twice Upon a Time* by Judy Sierra and Robert Kaminski (New York: H.W. Wilson, 1959), 33–44.

"Travels of a Fox" in *Great Children's Stories: The Classic Volland Edition* written and illus. by Frederick Richardson (Chicago: Rand McNally, 1972), 16–26.

Collections and Books of Creative Dramatics Advice:

Look What Happened to Frog: Storytelling in Education by Pamela J. Cooper and Rives Collins (Scottsdale, Ariz.: Gorsuch Scarisbrick, 1992). See Chapter Six "Story Dramatization: The Six P's."

Twice Upon a Time: Stories to Tell, Retell, Act Out and Write About by Judy Sierra and Robert Kaminski (New York: H.W. Wilson, 1989). Folktales retold in an easy-to-tell format. Suggestions for creative dramatics and other extensions of the story.

World Tales for Creative Dramatics and Storytelling by Burdette S. Fitzgerald (Englewood Cliffs, N.J.: Prentice-Hall, 1962). See Chapter 1, "Creative Dramatics."

Baby Rattlesnake's First Rattle

A Pawnee Tale

Thanks to Lynn Moroney for introducing us to this story
in her delightful picture book *Baby Rattlesnake.*

Baby Rattlesnake was sooo little.
He was sooo little he didn't even have a rattle yet.
Baby Rattlesnake wanted a *rattle*.

He went to Momma Rattlesnake.
      "Momma! Momma! I want a rattle!
      Give me a rattle!"

      "No, Baby Rattlesnake.
      You are too little.
      You would get into trouble with a rattle."

He went to Poppa Rattlesnake.
      "Poppa! Poppa! I want a rattle!
      Give me a rattle!"

      "No, Baby Rattlesnake.
      You are too little.
      You would get into trouble with a rattle."

Baby Rattlesnake went to Grandma Rattlesnake.
      "Grandma! Grandma! I want a rattle!
      Please give me a rattle!"

      "Baby Rattlesnake, you are too little.
      You would just get into trouble."

Baby Rattlesnake went to Grandpa Rattlesnake.
      "Grandpa! Grandpa! I want a rattle!
      Please please ! Give me a rattle!"

"No, Baby Rattlesnake.
You are too little.
You would get into trouble with a rattle."

But Baby Rattlesnake would not quit.
"*Please* Grandpa!
Please!
I am *really* big now.
Let me have my own rattle."

People got tired of hearing him whine.
Finally the elders said,
"Go ahead and give him a rattle.
He will just get into trouble.
But he will learn."

Baby Rattlesnake was *so* happy with his new rattle.
He sang a Rattlesnake Song.
"chhh…chhhh…chhh
chhh…chhhh…chhh"

He did a Rattlesnake Dance.
"chh…chh…chh…chh…
chh…chh…chh…chh…"

He was playing all over the place with his new rattle.

"chhhhh…chhhhh…
chhhhh…chhhhh…"

Then Baby Rattlesnake had an idea.
"I can *scare* somebody with my rattle!"

There was Jack Rabbit hopping down the road.
Baby Rattlesnake hid behind the rock.
He waited. He waited. He kept real still.
Hop…hop…hop…hop…

"*Chhhhhhhhh*!"
That Baby Rattlesnake *jumped* out rattling.
"*Help*!" Jack Rabbit jumped *so* high!
Baby Rattlesnake *laughed*.
"That was a good joke!
Who else can I scare?"

Here came Old Man Turtle.
> "Oh boy! I can scare him too!"

Baby Rattlesnake hid behind his rock.

Old Man Turtle came down the road.
So slow.
> "One foot.
> One foot.
> One foot.
> One foot."

Baby Rattlesnake waited.
He kept real still.
> "One foot.
> One foot.
> One foot…"

> "*Chhhhhhhhhh!!!!!*"

> "*Help!*"

Old Man Turtle jumped *so* high in the air.
Baby Rattlesnake *laughed* and *laughed*.
> "That was a good joke I played on Old Man Turtle.
> Who else can I scare?"

There was the Chief's Daughter coming down the road.
She walked so tall.
She held her head high in the air.
> "I can scare the Chief's Daughter!"

Baby Rattlesnake hid behind his rock.
He waited.
He kept real still.

The Chief's Daughter came down the road.
> *Step* and *step*.
> *Step* and *step*.

The Chief's Daughter was proud.
The Chief's Daughter was brave.
She was not afraid of *anything*.
> *Step* and *step*.
> *Step* and…

"Chhhhhhhh!!!!!!"

That Chief's Daughter whirled.
    "Ho!"
That Chief's Daughter brought her foot down *hard*
on Baby Rattlesnake's new rattle!
    "Ha!"
That Chief's Daughter ground his rattle into the path.
    Step and *step*.
    Step and *step*.

That Chief's Daughter walked on down the path.

    "ooooooohhhhhh…"
Poor Baby Rattlesnake crawled home.

Momma saw his broken rattle.
    "He was too young."

Poppa saw his broken rattle.
    "He was too young."

Grandma saw his broken rattle.
    "He was too young to have a rattle."

Grandpa saw his broken rattle.
    "So did you learn something, Baby Rattlesnake?
    Now don't ask for a rattle again.
    Not until you are old enough to know how to behave!"

And Baby Rattlesnake did not.

Tips for telling:

I like to use a maraca when telling this story and shake it whenever Baby Rattlesnake uses his rattle. After the story I retell the tale, and we act it out. At the end of that story session, I pass out envelopes and we make rattling rattlesnakes to take home.

Instructions:

1. Put a few grains of popcorn into an 8½" envelope. Seal the envelope.
2. Fold the envelope in half lengthwise. Shake the grains to one end.
3. Fold over the "tail" of the envelope, being careful to shake all of the grains into the "tail."
4. Staple the "tail" at the fold. This secures the grains within the folded over "tail."

5. Draw snake stripes on the envelope, add stick-on dots for eyes.
6. Shake your rattlesnake.

About the story:

This story was in the repertoire of Chickasaw teller Te Ata. The story is Pawnee and Lynn Moroney speculates that it may have been acquired from a Pawnee singer with whom Te Ata toured Chautauqua's in the 1920s. Lynn and Te Ata published the story as *Baby Rattlesnake* (San Francisco: Children's Book Press, 1989). Another version is found in "Pawnee Music" by Frances Densmore in the *Smithsonian Bureau of American Ethnology, Bulletin 93* (1929), 107-8. The version used here was developed by Margaret Read MacDonald and Wajuppa Tossa as a teaching tale for students in northeastern Thailand and was published there in *Storytelling as a Means of Preservation of Language and Culture and in the Process of Teaching and Learning* (Mahasarakham: Mahasarakham University, 1997), 84–88. The retelling both in Thailand and here appears with the permission of Lynn Morony. This retelling is clearly inspired by her picture book, which is excellent, reads aloud well, and can be used as a source to learn for storytelling itself. My version simply elaborates beyond the boundaries possible in a picture book. But be sure to see the picture book, too, before you begin telling. I sometimes tell the story first, and then read aloud the briefer version in the book, showing the pictures, then retell as we act it out.

Motif *J2131 Numskull injured.* *J2131.02 *Baby Rattlesnake scares passerby. Chief's daughter stomps on him.*

Tom Thumb's Wedding

A Folktale from Italy

Crystal Rooster woke up and began to crow
>"COCK-A-DOODLE-DOOO…
>What a fine summer morning!"

Crystal Rooster began to strut up and down in front of his house.
>"COCK-A-DOODLE-DOOOO…"

There on the road lay a letter.
>"What is *this*?'

Crystal Rooster picked it up.
>"Whatever does it say?
>C…R…Y…S…
>T…A…L…
>Crystal!
>That's MY name."

Crystal Rooster spelled out some more letters.
>"R…O…O…S…
>T…E…R…
>Rooster!
>Crystal Rooster!
>This must be for *me*!"

Carefully he read out the whole letter.
It said:
>"'CRYSTAL ROOSTER,
>CRYSTAL HEN,
>COUNTESS GOOSE,
>GOLDFINCH BIRDIE,
>YOU ARE INVITED TO TOM THUMB'S WEDDING.'

>"I am invited to a *wedding*!
>Excellent!
>There is always good food at a wedding.

There will be singing.
There will be dancing.
I am going to *go*."
Crystal Rooster started right off marching down the road.
He was so happy to be going to Tom Thumb's wedding.
He was clacking his beak, flapping his wings,
and singing:
"Clak...clak...clakkety-clak.
Flap...flap...flappety-flap.
I'm going to Tom Thumb's wedding.
I'm going to Tom Thumb's wedding."

Soon he met a hen.
"Buon Giorno, Crystal Rooster.
Where are you going so happily?"

"I am going to Tom Thumb's wedding."

"A wedding!
There will be lots of good food at a wedding.
There will be singing.
There will be dancing,
I will go, too!"

"No. No," said Crystal Rooster.
"You have to have an *invitation*.
I have one right here.
My name is written on it."

"Maybe my name is on it, too.
Would you look?
Look and see."
So Crystal Rooster unfolded the invitation and read it out:
"'CRYSTAL ROOSTER,
CRYSTAL HEN...'"

"That's *me*! That's *me*!
Crystal Hen! That's *me*!"

"Well then, you can go, too.
What fun!"
So Crystal Rooster and Crystal Hen went down the road.
"Clak-clak-clakkety-clak.

Flap-flap-flappety-flap.
We're going to Tom Thumb's wedding!
We're going to Tom Thumb's wedding!"

Soon they met a goose.
"*Buon Giorno*, Crystal Hen.
Buon Giorno, Crystal Rooster.
Where are you going so happily?"

"We are going to Tom Thumb's wedding!"

"A wedding?
There will be good food at a wedding.
There will be singing,
There will be dancing,
I will go, too!

"No. No. You have to have an *invitation*.
We have one right here.
Our names are written on it."

"Maybe my name is on there, too.
Can you read it?
Look and see if it has my name, too."

So Crystal Rooster unfolded the letter and read it out:
"'CRYSTAL ROOSTER,
CRYSTAL HEN,
COUNTESS GOOSE...'"

"Countess Goose?
That's *me*!
That's *me*!
I can go *too*!"

"Well, come along then!"

And the three started down the road.
"*Clak-clak-claketty-clak.*
Flap-flap-flappety-flap.
We're going to Tom Thumb's wedding!
We're going to Tom Thumb's wedding!"

Soon they met Goldfinch Birdie.
>*"Buon Giorno*, Crystal Rooster.
>*Buon Giorno*, Crystal Hen,
>*Buon Giorno*, Countess Goose.
>Where are you going so happily?"

>"We're going to Tom Thumb's wedding."

>"A wedding?
>I *love* weddings.
>There will be lots of food to eat.
>There will be singing.
>There will be dancing.
>I will come with you."

>"No. No. You have to have an *invitation*.
>We have one.
>Our names are written right here."

>"Isn't *my* name written, too?
>Look and see! Look and see!"

So Crystal Rooster unfolded the letter once more and began to
read:
>"'Crystal Rooster,
>Crystal Hen,
>Countess Goose,
>Goldfinch Birdie…'"

>"Goldfinch Birdie?
>That's *me*! That's *me*!
>I can go, *too*!"

>"Wonderful!
>Then off we go!"
And the four friends started happily down the road.
>*"Clak-clak-claketty-clak.*
>*Flap-flap-flappety-flap.*
>We're going to Tom Thumb's wedding!
>We're going to Tom Thumb's wedding!"
Until they met a *fox*.
>*"Buon Giorno*, my fine feathered friends.
>Where are you tasty morsels going so happily?"

"We're going to Tom Thumb's wedding."

"A wedding?
I love weddings.
I will go with you."

"No. No. You must have an invitation.
Our names are right here on this paper.
We are *invited*."

"I expect *my* name is on that paper, too."

"I don't think so," said Crystal Rooster.

"*Read* it and we will see," said Fox.

So Crystal Rooster read once more.
"'CRYSTAL ROOSTER,
CRYSTAL HEN,
COUNTESS GOOSE,
GOLDFINCH BIRDIE,
YOU ARE INVITED TO TOM THUMB'S WEDDING.'
No. Nothing there about a *fox*.
You can't go."

"But I *want* to go," said Fox.
"And what I want I *get*.
Give me a tail feather."
And snatching one of Crystal Rooster's long tailfeathers,
the fox used it as a pen and scratched onto the paper:
F...O...X
"See, *there* it says, 'Fox.'
Now let's *go*."

So the four friends and Fox went down the road.
Crystal Rooster lead the way,
Crystal Hen followed,
Countess Goose followed Crystal Hen,
and Fox brought up the rear.
But Goldfinch Birdie flew from tree to tree.
"Clak-clak-clakkety-clak.
Clak-clak-clakkety-clak.
Flap-flap-flappety-flap.

Flap-flap-flappety-flap.
We're going to Tom Thumb's wedding!
We're going to Tom Thumb's wedding!"

Suddenly Fox said to Countess Goose,
"I'm *hungry*.
Where is *lunch?*"

"There is no lunch.
We will eat at the wedding."

"But I'm hungry *now!*"
And Fox opened his huge jaws
and *swallowed* Countess Goose.

The friends had no idea Countess Goose was gone.
"Clak-clak-clakkety-clak.
Clak-clak-clakkety-clak.
Flap-flap-flappety-flap.
Flap-flap-flappety-flap.
We're going to Tom Thumb's wedding!
We're going to Tom Thumb's wedding!"

Fox came up behind Crystal Hen.
"I'm *hungry*.
Where is *lunch?*"

"There is no lunch.
We will eat at the wedding."

"But I am hungry *now!*"
Fox opened his huge jaws
and swallowed Crystal Hen.

Crystal Rooster did not hear a thing.
He marched happily on.
"Clak-clak-clakkety-clak.
Clak-clak-clakkety-clak.
Flap-flap-flappety-flap.
Flap-flap-flappety-flap.
We're going to Tom Thumb's wedding!
We're going to Tom Thumb's wedding!"

"Where is *lunch*?" said Fox to Crystal Rooster.

"There is no lunch.
We will eat after the wedding."

"But I am hungry *now*!"
Fox opened his huge jaws wide
and swallowed Crystal Rooster
...tail feathers and all.

"Goldfinch Birdie," called Fox.
"Come down here a moment
Where is *lunch*?"
Goldfinch Birdie turned around.
He saw a fox with a huge tummy.
He didn't see any of his friends.
The fox's tummy was bumping and thumping.
It sounded like something inside that tummy was calling,
"Help...help...get us out!"

"Oh, *my*. That fox has eaten my friends!"
Goldfinch Birdie thought quickly.
He flew down near Fox,
but not *too* near.
"If you are hungry for lunch, just follow me.
I will show you lunch."

Goldfinch Birdie flew ahead of Fox.
He led him straight to the field where the farmhands were working,
"Now watch, Fox.
Here comes the farmer's wife with lunch for the workers.
I will fly around her head and confuse her.
She will drop her lunch basket, and *you* can eat it all!"

"Excellent idea!" said Fox.
And to himself he added,
"And then I can eat Goldfinch Birdie for dessert!"

Goldfinch Birdie flew up to the farmer's wife.
He buzzed around her head.
"Stop that! Stop that, you silly bird!"
She dropped the basket of lunch
and ran after Goldfinch Birdie.

Fox began at once to gorge himself on the food.

But as soon as Fox was busy stuffing himself,
Goldfinch Birdie turned and flew back to the lunch basket.
The farmer's wife saw that fox eating the food!
> "Men! Men! Come quick with your hoes!
> This *fox* is stealing your lunch!"

Those farmhands ran so quickly.
They pounded that fox until he was senseless.

Then Goldfinch Birdie flew down and began to peek at the fox's
  stuffed tummy.
> "CHEEP! CHEEP! CHEEP!"

The farmhands looked more closely.
Inside the fox's tummy something was moving.
> "Let us out! Let us out! Let us out!"

Quickly the farmhands cut open the fox's belly.

Out came Crystal Rooster.
Out came Crystal Hen.
Out came Countess Goose.
What a mess they were!
They went right down to the stream and took a good bath.
Then they dried themselves in the sun.
They preened their feathers until were beautiful again.
Then off the four friends went to the wedding.
> *"Clak-clak-clakkety-clak.*
> *Clak-clak-clakkety-clak.*
> *Flap-flap-flappety-flap.*
> *Flap-flap-flappety-flap.*
> We're going to Tom Thumb's wedding!
> We're going to Tom Thumb's wedding!"

And when they got to the wedding...
what a feast they had!
There was good food.
There was singing,
There was dancing.
The party lasted all night long...
at Tom Thumb's wedding!

Tips for telling:

Children quickly learn to join in the birds' chant, *"Clak-clak-clakkety-clak."* The story is easy to act out; use as many roosters, hens, geese as you like. If working with very small children, you will need an adult accomplice to help the fox swallow the other children and stuff them away in a corner waiting for rescue.

About the story:

Another version of this story appears as "Crystal Rooster" in *Italian Folktales* by Italo Calvino (New York: Harcourt Brace Jovanovich, 1980), 360–61. This is a variant of *Z53 The animals with queer names: as hen (henny-penny), cock (cocky-locky), goose (goosey-poosey).* Thompson cites variants from England, Sweden, Denmark, Turkey, and the British West Indies.

12 Your Turn

NOW YOU HAVE TWENTY NEW STORIES TO PLAY WITH. Make them your own.

These stories can be told simply, sitting with your hands folded and speaking the tale quietly. Or they can be danced and drummed while surrounded with leaping children. There is no *right* way to tell these tales. The way *you* tell them will be just right for that moment.

The important thing is that you take to your heart some of these stories. These tales have delighted listeners in so many other times and places. Now it is your turn to pass them on.

And please don't get the notion that such playful stories are only for children. *Adults* like to play too! Just give them a chance!